"We have to convince them this is what we want. That we met when you first arrived, and that we were already engaged."

"But I only arrived a few days ago!"

"Never heard of love at first sight?"

Did she? Had she felt it, too? That crackle of connection…

Don't be an idiot. It wasn't love. It was lust.

Diego believed in lust. Passion even. Love? He didn't believe in love anymore. Couldn't. Not when he knew how the world really worked.

"When the men come back in again, make sure the diamond hits the light. They need to see the ring."

Isla pursed her lips, looked at her hand then nodded, tendrils of her auburn hair masking her expression. He pulled his fingers into a fist, willing them not to tease a few of her wayward curls into submission.

She sniffed and shook her hair back as if she was annoyed at his choice of paint for their new living room, rather than being thrown into the vortex of fear and confusion most people would have been in if their lives depended upon marrying a complete stranger.

Dear Reader,

Have you ever had a light bulb moment and run with it? That's what happened here with this book. A working title came to me (they are usually *wildly* unusable, which is why we have another lovely title for you to enjoy instead). It was "Married to the Mob Doc." Then I thought—what if our heroine had to marry said mob doc under duress? What on earth would make you marry someone you didn't know? I'm going to have to stop here, because the answer I dreamed up lies within these pages. I hope you find it as wild and romantic a ride as I did writing it. As ever, I love to hear from you all, so please don't be shy about getting in touch. I'm on Facebook and on Twitter, @AnnieONeilBooks.

xx *Annie O'*

THE DOCTOR'S MARRIAGE FOR A MONTH

ANNIE O'NEIL

HARLEQUIN® MEDICAL ROMANCE™

Recycling programs
for this product may
not exist in your area.

ISBN-13: 978-1-335-64144-1

The Doctor's Marriage for a Month

First North American Publication 2019

Copyright © 2019 by Annie O'Neil

Printed in U.S.A.

www.Harlequin.com

Books by Annie O'Neil

Harlequin Medical Romance

Single Dad Docs
Tempted by Her Single Dad Boss

Hope Children's Hospital
The Army Doc's Christmas Angel

Hot Greek Docs
One Night with Dr. Nikolaides

Italian Royals
Tempted by the Bridesmaid
Claiming His Pregnant Princess

Paddington Children's Hospital
Healing the Sheikh's Heart

Hot Latin Docs
Santiago's Convenient Fiancée

Christmas Eve Magic
The Nightshift Before Christmas

The Monticello Baby Miracles
One Night, Twin Consequences

London's Most Eligible Doctor
Her Hot Highland Doc
Her Knight Under the Mistletoe
Reunited with Her Parisian Surgeon

Visit the Author Profile page
at Harlequin.com for more titles.

This one goes to my editor, Laurie, who I finally get to work with after she spotted me in a So You Think You Can Write competition many moons ago. Thanks to her, my confidence grew enough to keep on trying, keep on writing and, eventually, get my very first contract to write books for Harlequin. Thank you so much, Laurie! Your faith in me has led to a whole magical world of book writing I never thought would come my way! xx Annie O'

CHAPTER ONE

"NO TAKERS FOR the Nocturnal Turtle Tour?" asked Isla MacLeay as she scrubbed at her face, hoping her father couldn't see that it was, as it had been for the past three days, stained with tears.

"Not tonight. I thought we had some takers, but…" Her father looked out at the huge expanse of beach before them. "I guess getting the sanctuary established is going to be a bit more of a task than I thought. Here you are, lassie."

She felt one of her father's soft cotton handkerchiefs brush against her hand. She took it with a smile she knew didn't reach her eyes as her heart cinched tight. It was the second time this week he'd acted like a "real dad."

If getting dumped a week before her wedding was all it took to get his attention, she would've faked a wedding years ago.

Before her father had found her she'd been sitting against a palm tree, next to the little tote bag that held her diary and her increasingly eclectic pen collection, almost enjoying quietly sniffling away as silvery moonlight bathed the idyllic crescent of beach, where palm leaves murmured in the light breeze as the warm Caribbean sea lapped and teased at the pure white sand.

She'd come a long way from her little Scottish home in Loch Craggen, but tonight the beach had been as far as she'd been prepared to go.

She had kissed her father goodnight when he'd pulled out yet another one of his huge folders full of plans for the El Valderon Turtle Sanctuary and, not being sleepy, had strolled to the beach for a bit of a sob, leaving the low-slung buildings of the sanctuary behind her, and losing herself to the beautiful cove which they surrounded.

The billowing foam arcing atop the waves surging in from the Caribbean Sea reminded her of a delicate glass of fizz, just about to over-flow. Not that she was used to champagne being popped and poured at the drop of a hat. Her fiancé—her *ex*-fiancé—hadn't really been one to plump for that sort of thing. Not for her, anyway.

Remembering his words had fresh tears rolling down her freckled cheeks. Just in case she hadn't understood what *"I've fallen in love with someone else"* meant…he'd gone on to make it plain as day.

"How could I marry you? It wouldn't be fair. To either of us. Sorry, babes. Now that I've dipped my toe into the waters of life off Crag-

gen it's plain as day. I'm a world traveler. And, as much as it pains me to say it, you're a boring, rule-abiding, science nerd. It's just not my scene, darlin'. Ciao!"

Ciao?

The man had only flown to Italy once. He'd not even left the airport and now he was fluent?

Pffft. That showed her for falling for pretty words and a handsome face. She saw it now. Plain as the hand in front of her face. Kyle had only wanted someone reliable until something better came along. The next man she met and fell for would be a nerd through and through.

"There's nothing wrong with being reliable as a millstone."

When her grandmother had said it, it had sounded like a good thing.

When Kyle had said it she'd instantly heard the bell toll for the end of their marriage plans.

She couldn't help but wonder how others might have reacted—what people who were perky flight attendants in Europe might have been inclined to say.

Not that she'd met Kyle's new girlfriend. *Girlfriend!* But the rumor mill ran stronger than the mountain rivers that flowed into the inky depths of Loch Craggen. Apparently the new girlfriend was absolutely *adorable* and *soooo* sophisticated.

What was wrong with corduroy skirts, woolly

tights and hand-knitted jumpers? It was *cold* in Loch Craggen. Even in August.

Which was precisely why she had packed just about nothing appropriate for her last-minute trip El Valderon. Was there *anything* appropriate, apart from mourning clothes? She wasn't mourning Kyle, exactly. But she did feel she was mourning the loss of something intangible. Either way, she needed new clothes and had promised to take herself shopping. One of these days.

Pop! Pop! Pop!

Startled into the present, she stared with her father out into the inky darkness as the moon slid behind a cloud.

"What was that?"

Despite the late-night tropical heat, goose bumps rippled up Isla's arms, then shot down her back.

It wasn't a sudden chill she felt.

It was fear.

She pressed her fingers to her eyes, gave them a quick rub, then pinged them open, forcing herself to adjust to the inky darkness.

"Dad?" She couldn't see him. He'd been right beside her a second ago!

Fear clashed with an age-old anger. Had he run off toward the danger, instead of staying with her when she truly needed him?

She squinted out into the darkness.

The gunfire sounded again.

"Dad? Daddy! Are you all right?"

Where *was* he?

Her heart pounded against her chest. Isla hadn't called her father "daddy" in years. Decades, even. At thirty-one years old she was a grown woman. A *doctor*. But fear had a way of reducing a girl to her essential self. A little girl who'd come halfway round the world to seek solace from her father when her heart had been smashed into a thousand little pieces.

None of that mattered now.

An anguished male scream broke through the roar of blood in her head as rapid-fire Spanish was lobbed from one end of the cove to the other.

She didn't have to be a doctor to know the sound of pain, but she was thanking heaven that she was. It narrowed her focus. Pushed away the fear. Gave her something to do: *help*.

She spun round and saw a young man clutching his shoulder. Her heart lurched into her throat. She saw blood pouring between his fingers. Oh no. He'd been hit.

Everything slowed down, as if she were in a frame-by-frame film sequence.

The atmosphere at the oceanside cove had flipped from tranquil to chaotic in little more than the blink of an eye. One minute she'd been quietly sobbing her heart out about her wreck of a life and the next… Gunfire and shouting erupted from each of the two heavily armed groups facing off against each other.

So these were the men her father had said "might bear a bit of a grudge" against the sanctuary.

The man stumbling toward her must have been caught in the crossfire between The El Valderon Turtle Sanctuary's security guards and the tattooed, slick-haired members of Noche Blanca—the ragtag but reportedly vicious, mafia-type group led by the island's one notorious criminal: Axl Cruz.

He had been enraged when the owners of a large coffee plantation had donated the land to the sanctuary. Her father had hinted that there had been a rise in tension over precious turtle eggs. Precious to Axl Cruz because they meant money on the black market. Precious to her father because the sea creatures were endangered.

Instinct set her in motion.

Flashes of gunfire lit up the inky black sky. An illustration, if she needed one, of why the so-called gang called themselves White Night.

Her nostrils stung with the sour scent of spent gunpowder.

A volley of Spanish came at her from all directions as yet another round of gunfire broke through the night. When the moon reappeared she saw her father.

"Daddy!"

Why were they dragging him away?

"I'm all right, love." Her father's scratchy brogue carried across the cove. "Just stay calm. You'll be fine. They only want the eggs. They won't hurt you if you do what they say. All right, laddies. *¡Suéltame!*"

She strained to hear her father's calm, ever-scientific voice rising and falling, explaining something in Spanish as calmly as if the gun-wielding *pandilleros* had come along for one of her father's nocturnal sea turtle tours.

Ever since her mum had died the man had lived on another planet. How else could one unbelievably intelligent human think he could talk down a criminal gang intent on illegal turtle egg sales?

It was why her grandmother had raised *her* to be the sensible one. The reliable one.

The boring one.

She pushed aside her ex's cruel words and tried to follow her father's directions. As bonkers as he was, there wasn't a chance on earth she was going to lose him too. Not after the week she'd had. So she did what she was good at: following protocol.

There was a gunshot victim and he needed help. *Now.*

She astonished herself by offering a polite smile to one of the burlier men closing in on her. His pitch-black hair was pulled back in a tight ponytail. If he loosened his hair and put on a smile she could imagine him as a father or son.

He grunted and looked away.

Apparently smiles weren't going to help tonight.

Her father had told her that in a good year on the black market a family could live for a year on the proceeds of a single night's haul of the precious eggs. Little wonder some of the men had turned to crime when the land had become protected.

Not protected well enough.

Her father's project was meant to put an end to the need for violence. Create a viable means of making a living on the island. Bring an end to the destruction of the endangered animals. An end to the violence. A way to legitimately support a family. But it would take time. Time these men didn't seem willing to give.

A tall, lanky man stepped forward and grabbed her arm as yet another unhooked a skein of rope from his shoulder.

Her vision blurred as reality dawned.

She was going to be held hostage.

She turned and caught a final glimpse of her father being manhandled toward the smattering of seaside bungalows where the sanctuary staff lived. Before he disappeared she heard him shouting something about calling for help.

An ice-cold flash of fear prickled along her spine.

Help? Which one of them was in any position to call for help? She'd only been on the island a few days, and those had largely been spent sobbing her eyes out over her broken engagement. The little girl in her wanted to scream with frustration. *He* was the one who was tapped into the local support network. *He* was the grown-up!

The male who'd been shot uttered a low groan as he dropped to his knees in pain.

And just like that she remembered she was an adult too. One with the power to help.

It felt as if hours had passed since she'd heard the first gunshots, but Isla knew better than most that only a few precious seconds had passed. Life-changing seconds.

The pony-tailed man shouldered an automatic weapon. She followed the trajectory of his gun as it swung to the far side of the cove.

He raised it to the starlit sky and fired. The sharp *rat-a-tat-tats* sounded more like a signal than an attempt to get the turtle sanctuary's rag-tag protection detail to run for the hills.

Her heart ached for the sanctuary security team. They were gentle men—cooks, farmers, bricklayers, fathers—whose sole desire was to see an end to the violence that threatened to taint their lives so cruelly.

Ire burnt and stung in her chest, then reformed as a white-hot rod of indignation. They shouldn't have to live like this. Fearing for their lives while trying to do the right thing by their families and their community.

"Everybody *stop*!"

Much to her astonishment, they did.

The moment's reprieve in the shooting and shouting gave her a chance to listen for anyone approaching or more instructions from her father.

Nope.

Not a living soul.

Just a chance to realize that her heart had stopped hammering against her rib cage as if it too were trying to escape.

Two weeks ago she would've been hiding under something right now. Most likely the big bed in her little stone cottage on Craggen. Not standing between two gun-toting groups of men with her arms out like some sort of bonkers traffic controller.

Was being dumped more character-building than soul-destroying? Or was the truth a bit more simple.

After the week she'd had Isla really didn't have time for this sort of ridiculous machismo.

She pushed her own issues to the wayside. Her father was here to *help* the community—not hinder. Nor had she faced up to a lifelong fear of flying only to get killed when she got here.

She was here to lick her emotional wounds, sulk a little. Wallow. Something she never did. And she was *not* best pleased to have to patch together gun-wielding turtle egg poachers just because they didn't see the sense in her father's big plan.

The same father, she reminded herself, who probably should've mentioned the fact that El Valderon was more akin to the Wild West of yesteryear than a restorative Caribbean spa.

Maybe he simply didn't want to see the dark side.

Her heart softened. For once, her father had been trying to do right by her. To give her a place to hide away from the prying eyes of Loch Craggen. Regroup after being deemed "the most boring girlfriend on earth."

Well, Kyle would've been boring too, if his mother had been killed and his father had lost the plot. *Someone* needed to be practical. *Someone* needed to look after Grannie. Someone had to *be there*.

Ponytail Man retrained his gun on her. She

stared him straight in the eye. Here was her chance to show Kyle Strout just what boring looked like.

She looked down at the pure white sand currently soaking up the splatterings of very real blood, courtesy of the egg poachers and guards shooting at each other.

A swift shot of resolve crackled through her like a flash of unexpected lightning.

She wasn't boring.

Nor was she going to engage in all this mopey, weepy, victim of an ill-fated romance palaver.

She was going to save this man's life, then find her father and help him make his dream of saving the sea turtle come true.

She squared off to Ponytail Man and fixed him with her fiercest look of determination. The type she would've given Annie Taggart's highly energized toddlers when she needed to take blood samples.

Yes, she'd show Kyle *precisely* how exciting "fifty shades of boring" could be.

Fury pumped through Diego's veins. He slammed his phone against the stucco wall outside the small hospital, not caring when the handset shattered.

If Noche Blanca were going to act like cavemen they could resort to smoke signals if they wanted his help.

But as quickly as the urge to tell them where to stick their call for help launched his blood pressure through the stratosphere, it crashed back down to earth.

A patient was a patient. Even if that patient was a class-A idiot. And this particular idiot was the son of Noche Blanca's take-no-prisoners head honcho Axl Cruz. If he died there was no telling the extremes Axl would take to exact revenge.

Diego picked up the pieces of his phone and shoved them into his pocket, shaking his head in utter disbelief. It was the third burner he'd obliterated in a week. Just yesterday, as he'd been stitching up one of Axl's *pandilleros* who'd lacerated his arm after putting his meaty fist through a window, he'd thought he'd made it crystal clear. The help would continue so long as they left the sanctuary alone.

Transition periods took time. And, sure, it depleted everyone's pocket money—which he knew was rich, coming from him—but the ultimate reward was peace. A steady economy for all the islanders. That was priceless. And it was why he'd instructed his family's company to gift the land to the sanctuary.

He swore as he strode into the hospital, not caring who heard.

"*Amigo!* Hold up."

He whirled round as the small hospital's head surgeon caught up to him.

"*Que paso?* I didn't think you were on tonight."

The thunderous expression on Diego's face told Dr. Antonio Aguillera all he needed to know.

He raised his hands and backed off. "I'll call in back-up."

"I've got it," Diego growled, grabbing a fresh pair of scrubs and a pair of surgical scrubs from a porter passing with a supplies trolley. "I'll bring them back to the clinic."

They both knew what that meant. These patients weren't on the right side of the law. The hospital was stretched to the limit as it was, and Diego knew more than most what happened when blood was shed and Noche Blanca were involved.

"Just a bit short on supplies." He'd ordered some in from the States, but, as often happened in developing countries, things went missing.

"Okay, brother. Good luck."

Anton disappeared into a nearby supplies cupboard and moments later handed Diego a jute coffee sack he knew would be stuffed full of supplies. Supplies that the hospital's administration would never officially hand over to him, despite the number of lives he'd saved that hadn't been linked to Noche Blanca.

Diego gave his colleague a slap on the back. One that communicated all the things he couldn't say.

No one will ever be able to replace my brother, but thank you for treating me like one. We both know luck counts for nothing when dealing with Noche Blanca.

"See you in the morning."

With any luck.

"Dr. Vasquez! *Momentito, por favor!*"

Irritation crackled through him. He didn't need to wriggle out of another administrative hoop. He wasn't on shift tonight.

He turned around.

Maria del Mar.

The woman was half siren, half business mogul. It was a shame she'd picked healthcare as her means of expressing the two sides of her personality.

Running the hospital was akin to a hot night in the sack for her. The life and death decisions… The status… The ability to play God… Or goddess, in her case.

The only reason he worked at the hospital was because he'd vowed not to hold the rest of the islanders accountable for one woman's idiot decision.

Sure. It sent a message to Noche Blanca. *You wield guns? Your problem.*

The only thing was, when it was your kid brother lines got blurred.

"No time, Maria." He tapped the face of his non-existent watch.

It was a ten-minute boat run to the turtle sanctuary. He'd thought with Professor MacLeay's plans to turn the turtle eggs into a legitimate commodity Noche Blanca might back off. That Axl would move on to another island, just as he had moved to theirs some fifteen years ago.

Maria wobbled toward him on her ridiculous high heels. Why the woman was even *at* the clinic after-hours was beyond him.

He snorted.

She has no life. Just like you.

No. That was exactly the point. He *did* have a life. Unlike his brother, who'd died just a few miles away from this very hospital.

Nico hadn't been a criminal. Wayward? Absolutely. But his heart had been pure gold. When some *bandilleros* from a neighboring island had tried to move in on El Valderon Nico had thrown himself between a bullet and the eldest son of Axl Cruz. On nights when he let himself think about it, Diego guessed his brother had thought *Better the devil they knew...*

In Maria's eyes the life-saving gesture had

painted Diego's kid brother with the Noche Blanca brush, and Nico had bled out a handful of miles away as an ambulance idled in the hospital's parking lot.

Would going there have been scary? Sure. But that was what bullet proof vests and the police were for. And most of Noche Blanca weren't true criminals. They were weak men, intimidated and bullied into a life of crime by someone who promised them untold riches. Riches he had no right to promise them.

The only good thing about Axl Cruz was that he liked a clean shop. Not one other gang had ever gained a foothold on their small island nation.

Better the devil they knew...

"Diego Vasquez! Where are you off to with a bag of El Valderon coffee beans?"

She knew as well as he did that the sack he was holding wasn't full of premium roast.

He slung it over his shoulder and pasted on his version of a good-boy smile. "Off to help a citizen of this fair isle, Maria. Where else?"

He never saw the point in lying.

"That citizen had better not be inked up and wearing knuckle dusters."

He gave a careless shrug. "Won't know till I get there."

Her eyes narrowed. "Who made the call?"

"A concerned citizen."

He knew the drill now. Keep it vague, then she couldn't say no. Theirs was an unwritten agreement, but to all intents and purposes it was written in stone. So long as he could use hospital supplies to treat patients on-scene he'd continue to work at the poorly staffed hospital. The second she turned off the supply room tap it would be *Hasta luego, mamacita.*

"Meet up after for a drink? Maybe we can talk about putting you on the roster for a few more shifts?"

He laughed. He had to hand it to her. If she wanted something she went for it. Her husband must have one helluva spine. Diego was civil to her. Polite, even. But there wasn't a chance on God's green earth that he would be her friend.

"I've got to go, Maria." He swung the bag back round. "Duty calls."

He pulled the keys to his motorboat from his pocket and set off at a jog. He wasn't going to let Maria stand in the way of yet another life being lost.

Not on his watch. Not ever again.

CHAPTER TWO

ISLA HAD TWO CHOICES.

Give in to the nerves that were threatening to consume her alive, proving Kyle right for dumping her and moving on to someone with "a bit more pizzazz, baby." Or she could make her parents proud.

She chose the latter.

Sure, her mother was no longer here to see her, and her father wasn't bearing *actual* witness—not to mention the fact she was saving a human versus an endangered species—but there were guns, bullet wounds and angry faces holding ground over invisible turf lines. This was the stuff her parents were known for.

Besides… These goons had her father.

Losing one parent was bad enough. And when her grandmother had passed away a couple of years back she'd been devastated. No way was she losing her father as well.

She wasn't ready to be an orphan.

"Are you going to let me go to him or not?" Isla glared at Scarface—her new nickname for

Ponytail Man who, now that he'd closed in on her, had revealed a raised scar running the length of his jawline.

There was some nice stitch work there for what looked like a massively botched job in the old "assassination with one stroke of the knife" department'. It looked more jig-jaggy than one-fell-swoopy. Whoever had done the surgery had done their best with what must have been a pretty horrific wound. Not to mention offering Scarface the preferred end of the stick in the whole staying alive thing. She'd like to meet that doctor if she got the chance.

Scarface snapped something short and staccato at her. It didn't sound very nice, and suffice it to say her nerves were shot.

"That's not much of a way to speak to a lady. Especially when she has plans to help your wee friend, here."

She pointed down toward the shoreline, trying to channel the strength and courage her mother had virtually glowed with.

"I'll have you know if that young man has an arterial bleed…" She crossed her arms and gave him her best knowing look. "He'll be dead by now. *Muerto*." She drew a line across her neck and made a dead face.

Scarface stepped forward, aimed his gun directly at her face and called the others to close in on her.

Oops.

She'd have to work on her communication by body language skills.

She shook her head and feigned world-weariness with a heavy sigh. "I am a doctor. *Médico.*" She pointed at herself again, hoping the word was an actual Spanish word.

She'd taken an oath to treat each and every patient who came her way. Even if they had been caught stealing turtle eggs for their alleged powers of sexual prowess.

Once Mr. Gunshot Wound was in Recovery, she'd make it clear to him that the one thing these eggs *did* produce was *turtles*—not a hot night in the sack. Unless, of course, he was iron deficient, in which case she could recommend some supplements.

See? Sensible and *sassy.*

She turned toward the young man. Instantly all the guns were lifted a bit higher. A metallic reminder that her freedom was not her own.

"I need to examine him," she said, irritation threading actively through her voice as she met another one of the *pandillero's* dark eyes.

No response.

"If I don't get to him he's going to die."

The men stared at her.

She persisted. "He could drown. Look at him!"

The poor lad was sprawled on the shoreline, legs apart, hands clutched to his chest, and the tide was coming in without an ounce of pity for a young man whose life could be taken away. Much like the baddie now staring at her as if he were carved out of marble.

This was absolute madness!

She glanced toward the security men wearing El Valderon Turtle Sanctuary T-shirts. Their guns had been taken from them and they were being tied to palm trees by yet more members of Noche Blanca. *Terrific.* When had *that* happened?

"Any one of you willing to let me know why I can't help this guy?"

She stared at Scarface for answers. He pushed her further into the center of the newly floodlit part of the cove with the butt of his rifle.

"Hey!"

She rubbed the small of her back. *No one—* and that included gun-wielding criminals trying to steal turtle eggs from idyllic beaches in the middle of the Caribbean—was going to push her around. Had she mentioned being dumped this week? The cancelled wedding?

She wheeled on him. "I am a doctor," she ground out. *"Dottore?"* She pointed at herself, wondering why she was now speaking in Italian.

Maybe because you're a boring GP whose only access to the world is via your television.

She pushed Kyle's cutting tone out of her head. It was a heck of a lot better than getting access to the world via an array of flight attendants' lady gardens!

She gave the pushy gunman her best no-nonsense face. The one she always had to use with Mrs. MacGregor when she refused to take her insulin. Scottish stubbornness was a force to be reckoned with. If she could get Mrs. Mac-Gregor to listen she could do the same with these men.

"I can stop your friend from bleeding to death…" she pressed her hands to her stomach and then braved making her dying face again before looking him in the eye "…but you have to let me go to him."

She pointed at the young man again, speaking as calmly as she could. Difficult with her heart trying to launch itself into her throat every few seconds.

"I need to *help* him."

She kept pointing at herself and then the young man, feeling about as awkward as she did every Christmas when her aunties forced her to play charades.

Talking slowly didn't appear to be remotely helpful. The man stared at her entirely unmoved.

He would have been terrific at playing a tree in the school play. She tried to picture the scene in an attempt to make him seem less scary. Miraculously, it worked.

So she did the only thing she could think of that would end this ridiculous stand-off while that poor man bled into the approaching surf. She ignored the man in front of her and began deliberately walking toward her patient.

No one moved a muscle.

No guns were raised.

No safety catches were unclipped.

Not that she really knew what that would sound like, but she was over-familiar with the crime show *oeuvre* and knew having the safety on or off was very important.

Was that what she'd done her life these past few years? Approach it with the safety on?

Well… Look at her now. Here she was in the middle of a crime scene, marching toward a patient as if the Hippocratic oath made her bullet proof.

At least if she died it would be in a blaze of glory. How very "MacLeay" of her. That would make the papers back home!

She looked down at her wrinkled eyelet blouse and crumpled A-line skirt. Her hand crept up to her hair. Her auburn curls had exploded into the equivalent of a comedy wig the second she'd stepped off the plane and she hadn't had the heart to try and wrestle them into submission. *Yet*. She'd given herself a week to cry and feel sorry for herself and she was only halfway through it.

Another reason to be annoyed with these *banditos*. How *dare* they interrupt her self-indulgent sob-fest when she so rarely took time for herself?

She gave her shoulders a little wriggle and kept her head held high. Looks weren't everything. Besides, she hadn't been shot yet, so perhaps dying in a scrappy skirt and T-shirt ensemble wouldn't be an issue.

She kept her eyes glued on the young man. A late teen at best. On the cusp of the rest of his life. He deserved a fighting chance to make some new decisions. Take a fresh path. And she was going to be the one to give him the chance. Then the *pandilleros* would free her, liberate her father, and everyone could get on with their lives.

Scarface shouted at her and then at another one of his *hombres* as the roar of a motorboat cracked through the thick night air. She heard the word *médico* somewhere in there, so thought the best thing to do was to keep on walking.

Finally! They were getting the hint. She was trying to *help*. And maybe the boat was the island version of an ambulance.

The waves were just beginning to shift the sand around the boy. She pulled off her light cardigan and moved his hands away from the wound without too much effort. His strength was clearly fading. She sucked in a sharp breath. The bullet had entered the lower region of his right shoulder. His breathing was jagged. She pressed her fingers to the pulse line on his throat. Accelerated.

Diagnoses flew threw her mind. Pneumothorax? Chest wall tenderness? Only an X-ray would give a proper read on the situation, but if that bullet had nicked the boy's lung on entry there was every chance he was suffering a hemo-pneumothorax. A potentially lethal combination of air and blood filling the chest cavity.

"Me llama, Isla."

He stared at her with glazed eyes and said nothing.

She silently berated herself. It didn't matter if he knew her name or not. What mattered was whether or not she could stop the bleeding and keep him breathing. The frightened look in his eyes sharpened her resolve to help him. Her heart twisted inside her chest as it hit home just how fortunate she had been as a child.

Okay, her parents had been away on research trips for the bulk of her childhood, but she'd had her grandmother. She'd known her parents would try their best to get home for holidays. They'd make a huge event out of her birthdays. She'd been clothed, fed, and she'd always known she was loved.

It was why she'd vowed to become such a solid rock for her father when her mother had died. She knew half of his world had been torn away from him that day and, like her grandmother before her, she was going to be there for him. Reliable. Dependable.

Boring.

She gave her head a shake. Boring or not, she had a patient.

"Isla," she repeated, pointing to herself. *"No hablo Española."*

Obviously. She'd hardly be prattling on to him in English if she was fluent in Spanish.

He said nothing.

"I'm here to help."

She did her best not to look horrified when she tore a bit of his shirt away to examine the open wound the bullet had made. You didn't get this sort of injury at her "humdrum fuddy-duddy" general practice on Loch Craggen. The worst she'd seen since she'd taken over from Old Doc Jimmy MacLean was an accidental impalement when a pitchfork-throwing contest had gone wrong.

She pressed her cardigan to the wound and as gently as she could turned the young man on to his side, so she could see if the bullet had come out the other side. No.

That scenario came with its own set of complications. Her mind whirled back to her first posting after med school. A central Glasgow A&E department. The gunshot and stabbing victims there had the entire Imaging Ward at their disposal. X-rays to locate the bullets. CT scans to check for symptoms, and any indication of vascular damage or unstable vital signs.

The only thing she wouldn't need here was an MRI. If that bullet was close to any vital soft tissue structures Magnetic Resonance Imaging was the last thing you wanted with a metal bullet inside you.

She pressed her fingers to the young man's carotid artery. *If he loses more blood...*

She gave her head a short, sharp shake. His pulse was still there. He was obviously a fighter. *Good.* He was too young to die and, judging by the impressive array of ink on his arms, and the fact he wasn't wearing the sanctuary uniform, she had a feeling that if he lost his life on her watch things might not pan out so well for her father.

She was mentally kicking herself for not bringing her medical kit on the trip. The only useful things she had back at the bungalow were an extra-large box of tissues, the small bottle of tequila she'd spied on her father's bookshelf and so far refused to let herself pinch, and her ever-present pair of tweezers.

She might be boring, but her eyebrows were perfect. Not to mention the fact she could pull a sliver out of a little boy's knee faster than you could say *boo*.

What she wouldn't give for a wound-packing kit.

What this kid needed was a hospital. And blood. An IV line chock-full of antibiotics. An X-ray and a chest tube to get the air out of his chest cavity and into his lungs.

As if on cue, a medium-sized motorboat roared into the isolated cove. A gabble of response burst from all the men who had been closing in round Isla.

When she clapped her eyes on the man at the helm of the high-tech boat—a man with inky dark hair, bone structure that would put a super-model to shame and body language that belonged solely to an elite group of alpha males she'd never even dreamed of seeing in real life, let alone meeting on a tropical beach—one thing and one thing only popped into her mind: *You're not to be trusted. Not by a long shot.*

Diego took in the scene as quickly as he could. Eight men circled around something or someone on the beach. The reason he'd been called, no doubt. Paz "Cruzito" Cruz. Axl's youngest son.

The pointlessness of it all clouded his heart.

A young man shouldn't be risking his life so another could slurp down raw turtle eggs in a pint of beer.

Axl told them they were brave. *Revolutionaries.* Taking what was rightfully theirs.

Cowards. That was what they really were.

Cowards with guns threatening an already poor nation with civil unrest.

He jumped out of the boat in one fluid motion, the warm sea water saturating his trousers up to his thighs. He pulled the motorboat up to the shore by a thick rope, which he tossed to one of the younger men. He threw his keys to another. They knew the consequences if anything happened to his boat.

Prison. For the lot of them.

But as it stood turning them in wasn't on the agenda. Saving a life was.

"Dónde está Cruzito?"

The men parted and there he was. The son of Noche Blanca's head honcho. Bleeding out on the beach over a handful of worthless cracked turtle eggs. They would've brought him maybe ten dollars. Twenty if he was lucky. Hardly the "big pull" he knew the kid was trying to reel in to win his father's approval.

He'd met him before. Cruzito was no career criminal. He was a boy trying to make his father proud the only way he knew how. The sooner he learnt that winning his father's approval was nigh on impossible, the better.

Diego bit back the telling-off the seventeen-year-old deserved. He'd save his life first. *Then* he'd give him a telling off. And hand him over to his father for an even bigger one.

His eyes traveled to the pair of hands pressing a blood-soaked wodge of fabric onto the gunshot wound. A woman's hands. Delicate. Pale skin. Creamy white and soft as silk. His gaze slid up her arms and widened when he reached her face.

His heart slammed against his rib cage so hard it punched the air straight out of his chest.

She was unlike any woman he'd ever seen. Utterly bewitching. Like some sort of fairy creature. The type who emerged from enchanted woodlands in faraway countries covered in snow and ice and had the power to take a man's heart hostage if she chose to.

Not that she looked cold-hearted. Far from it. Nor did she look as if she needed his help. Quite the opposite, in fact.

Her heart-shaped faced was a picture of crystalized concentration. Her cheeks were pinked up with exertion. Her richly colored auburn hair looked as though it was made out of a millions strands of coiled silk. Wild and untameable. When he met her bright blue eyes, sparking with life, he thought the exact same thing. Here was a woman who did things *her* way.

"Are you just going to stand there or are you going to use those long legs of yours to walk over here and help me?"

He absorbed the Scottish accent and connected the dots. Doug MacLeay's daughter. She had to be. Where the Professor had a *Let's all calm down and talk about this* approach, his daughter looked as though she were ready to spit fire.

Her eyes lasered across the collection of men who had now finally dropped their weapons. "No one here seems to have a polite bone in their body. I hope you're planning on breaking the mold. A medical kit and a fourteen or sixteen-gauge needle wouldn't go awry either."

He smiled. He liked being right. She *was* feisty. Just as quickly he sobered. Axl Cruz didn't give a flying monkey if the most beautiful woman on the island was tending to his son. She'd seen too much. Knew too much. Cruzito's wouldn't be the only life he'd have to save today. Just by being here this woman had started a clock to her inevitable assassination.

The tumble of curls masked her eyes as she tipped her head toward the shoreline. "Tell me that boat of yours goes to the hospital."

"No." He shook his head. "But I'm here to help. Diego Vasquez," he said, by way of introduction.

She rolled her eyes. "Well, get on with it, then. This flimsy jumper of mine's hardly going to save the lad's life, is it?"

The corners of his mouth twitched. Not the usual response he got. Usually it was more fawning. Sycophantic, even. More the swinging of a hip and the heave of a bosom if it was one of the island's few socialites. A batting of the eyes if it was that petite curvy nurse in Pediatrics.

He kind of liked being huffed at. But he liked saving lives more.

He rattled through a swift set of instructions in Spanish that set the men running.

In under a minute a stretcher was pulled out of the back of the boat, along with a wound-packing kit, a catheter and a chest tube.

He switched to English. "You're a doctor?"

She nodded. "Dr. MacLeay. Doug MacLeay's daughter. Isla."

Isla. "A beautiful name for a beautiful woman."

They both cringed at the cheesy line, but he wasn't about to take it back. In just a handful of seconds she'd lit fires inside his gut he'd long thought dormant. Dead, even. Dead for a very precise reason. Relationships meant caring. And caring meant loss.

He didn't do loss. Not anymore.

"I hope you've got a wound pack in there. I can't tell if the bullet's hit anything. Increased blood pressure and respiratory rate indicate the lung's taken a nick, or perhaps a bit of bone from the rib cage is lodged in there." She gave her shoulders a little shrug up to her ears.

He knew the drill. All too well, unfortunately.

He pulled out a handful of gauze packs. His hands covered hers as they swiftly packed the wound together.

He ignored the fireworks shooting up his arms and arrowing south as he spoke. "I've got a couple of IV bags preloaded with antibiotics in my run-bag. Looks like he'll need them. *Now.*"

She dropped her lids to half-mast over those bright blue eyes of hers, sucked in a sharp breath and pulled her hands away from his, dousing them in the approaching surf. Neither of them watched the blood travel back into the sea as the wave withdrew into the ocean.

"First…"

She pulled an IV bag from his medical tote, squinted at the writing on it, nodded, then expertly inserted a needle into Cruzito's arm. She connected it to the removable plug, then filled the drip chamber as she held the IV bag pinched between her shoulder and chin while he continued to compress the wound. Once she'd purged the air from the line she opened the catheter port so the solution could begin to flow.

"I hope you have a supply of O-positive blood in that bag somewhere. And second—I'm not going anywhere without my father."

"It's probably best if you leave him out of it."

"My only living relative?" Outrage radiated from her every pore. "I don't bloody think so!"

Diego lowered his voice. "If he's hiding, just leave him there. It's safest."

Giving the family land to the sanctuary had seemed like such a good idea. Now it seemed like his worst.

Life is complicated. Peace takes time. Peace takes perseverance.

"Too late for that," Isla bit back. "Two of your mates strong-armed him out of here. I want to see him before I do anything else." She held up the IV bag. "An air embolism is a dangerous thing for a man already teetering between life and death."

Something told him there wasn't a chance on earth she would really compromise Cruzito's welfare. If she really would take a life for a life she wouldn't have been compressing his wound with five gun barrels pointing at her head. Only a doctor who took her vow of care seriously would be kneeling in the blood-stained surf, prepared to give life to a man who was responsible for her father being dragged away by armed gang members.

Diego knew he wielded enough power with the thugs that all he had to do was say the word and they would pull her away. Disappear her. But he couldn't load Cruzito into his boat and get on with things without his conscience bashing him in the head every five seconds. She was fighting for her family. And that spoke to him louder than anything else could.

He turned to El Loco. *"Donde esta el Profesor?"*

El Loco, the largest of the group replied. They had him "in custody." El Jefe had rung when he'd heard about Cruzito and wanted "a word".

Diego's eyebrows shot up. A "word" could easily be accompanied by a bullet, followed by a mysterious disappearance.

This was his fault. *He* should be the one having a word. He hadn't told anyone he was the one who had donated the land. Most people thought it was government property and, as such, would remain unfunded. Noche Blanca hadn't realized until he'd got here that Doug MacLeay had come with more than his heart on his sleeve. He'd come with money. And the means to change the power structure on the island.

"Hello? Excuse me?" Isla MacLeay was waving a hand in front of his face. "I don't suppose you have any oxygen in that magic bag of yours? His respiratory distress is increasing."

Diego produced a small tank and deftly slipped the mask over Cruzito's mouth and nose.

"And can I get that fourteen-gauge? I don't think the chest tube can wait."

"I don't have any one-way valves on me. Just the catheter hub." He opened his case, his hand automatically going to it.

"Do you have a pair of gloves?"

"Yes," he said, passing them to her.

He watched as she deftly slipped the needle into the second intercostal space, then asked for a scalpel, surprising him when she cut the finger off one of the gloves, inserted it on top of the catheter hub and heaved a sigh of relief when it began to flutter as the air released and Cruzito's gasping eased.

Impressive. The woman knew how to improvise. It was one of his specialties and he hadn't seen that particular technique before.

Diego lowered his voice and tried to make it look as if he was speaking to Isla about treating Cruzito.

"Do you know how things work here? With Noche Blanca?"

"I'm getting a pretty good idea."

And she clearly wasn't impressed. What she should have been was scared. Her father's life was in danger. Hers too. There was nothing win-win about this situation. The only way he could keep her alive for now was to make her crucial to Cruzito's welfare.

"Help me bind this packing for the bullet entry wound and we'll get him on the boat."

It wasn't a request.

She met his gaze, seemed to understand what he was saying and gave him a curt nod. She put the IV back between her chin and shoulder, then wound the gauze round Cruzito's shoulder as Diego carefully raised him and held him steady so Isla could tightly secure the gauze in place.

He continued in a low voice. "Have you seen El Jefe?"

She shook her head no.

"He's The Chief. The man who runs Noche Blanca. This is his son."

Her shoulders stiffened but she continued to wrap. Most people would have run for the hills or broken down in tears. She took the information in silently.

She was obviously running on adrenaline. He knew the feeling all too well.

He'd been in her shoes seven long years ago, but he could still remember every second of that night as if it had just happened.

He swallowed back the memories and continued, "They've run the island for the past ten years or so."

"Is this a turf war? Are there other gangs they're fighting with?"

"No. It's… There's a complicated history on El Valderon. All of the islands round here—like tiny countries…" He paused and started again. "You know how a farmer likes to 'know' his fox?"

"What? Keep the fox sweet otherwise a meaner, bigger one will move in?"

"Precisely. That's how it works here. There are other gangs who are much worse over in Latin America. Much more violent. This…" He nodded toward the hodgepodge squad of henchmen. "This is small-fry."

He watched as she absorbed the information. Many visitors refused to understand. Couldn't comprehend how might ruled over right. Especially on such a small island with a population under a million.

But fear, power and a very clear identity were effective means of gaining control. It was the way they'd won over his kid brother. A reedy teenager who hadn't yet found his place in the world. They'd given him one. Then put him in the line of fire.

Diego didn't know who he loathed more. The hospital for not treating him, Noche Blanca for putting him in front of a bullet, or himself for not seeing what was happening and forcing his brother to work for the family business.

He'd turned his loathing into action. Volunteering to treat any victim of violence, wherever they were, no matter the circumstances. No matter the danger.

"Your father's ruffled a lot of feathers since he's arrived here." He met her solid gaze. *Damn.* He'd never known eyes to be so blue. Or so unwavering in their ability to meet his. "You don't look surprised. I'm guessing you're your father's daughter."

She huffed out a laugh. "Genetically? Yes."

An invisible knife plunged into his gut and began to carve upwards toward his heart. Isla shouldn't have to go through what he had. Endure the loss senseless violence could bring.

He tilted his chin up at El Loco—the universal man signal for *Hey, pal, tune in.*

In Spanish he asked if he could find out if El Jefe would bring Isla's father to the clinic. The one hidden away from prying eyes.

"Estas loco?" The enormous bodyguard who had been with the gang since he'd been a teenager looked shocked.

"Sí." He shrugged, as if asking for the impossible was just how he rolled.

It *was* crazy. But if Diego saved Cruzito, Noche

Blanca would owe him a second favor. And he was going to call both of those favors in tonight.

"Call him."

He flicked his head at the other men and issued a few quick instructions. They began forming a chain to load Cruzito onto the boat. He fixed his gaze on Isla.

"You ready for the ride of your life?"

Her jawline tightened and she arched an eyebrow. "Ready when you are."

CHAPTER THREE

ISLA WAS DISCOVERING new things about herself at a rate of knots. Riding in a motorboat and willing a gunshot victim who was patently on the side of the "baddies" to survive apparently did that to a girl. If this boy didn't make it… It wasn't worth thinking about. Seven years of medical training had brought her to this point. And the revelations were flying thick and fast.

First and foremost: she'd do anything to save her father's life. Including volunteering to help Diego with the young teen's surgery—a skill-set she had proactively stepped away from when she'd moved to Loch Craggen.

Which was how she now found herself in a well-kitted-out surgical suite tucked at the back of an inauspicious bungalow. All right. She'd been asked to help with the surgery. And it hadn't strictly been a "request' as such—more like a *I'd strongly advise participating if you want to your father to survive this sorry mess.* But…all things considered…she hadn't done emergency medicine in ages and she was pretty pleased with how it was all coming back.

Like riding a bike, her father would have said. With scalpels and suture kits and heart-rate monitors, but yes.

On the flipside, with Diego always within a meter's reach she didn't know whether she felt protected or as if she were being lured into another charming man's web of lies. Like a Caribbean Stockholm syndrome. The worst possible antidote to her broken engagement. Her shattered confidence. The terror careering through her frayed nerves.

She glanced at Diego. Most of his face was hidden behind a mask, apart from his espresso-brown eyes outlined with kohl-black lashes. Were those eyes to be trusted? Were they really the key to a man's soul?

There'd been a magnetic flash of connection when they'd met, and it hadn't been the kind that repelled. It had been a primal response that had felt completely out of her control. At this exact moment her body's heightened sensitivity to anything and everything Diego seemed the scariest part of this whole palaver.

And that started with wearing scrubs that were patently Diego-sized. Rolled up at the ankles. Super-roomy over the shoulders.

It wasn't simply wearing the man's clothes that

had her body super-alert to the brush and swoosh of the cotton against her belly, her breasts. It was that they were meant for *him*. A man she didn't know was friend or foe. And she had literally put herself in everything but his shoes.

It was an entirely unwelcome intimacy and her body was squirming with discomfort. No one wanted to walk in the shoes of their father's murderer.

It definitely wasn't his fresh-off-the-runway looks that were disarming her. Not by a long shot. It was his ease with her. With *them*. With this whole situation.

Not creepy. Or scary. More…*caring*. Reassuring. It had to be a clever ruse to disarm her. Just as her ex had lavished her with praise for being solid, steady, reliable, and then at the first sniff of something more interesting left her in the lurch.

Trust, suffice it to say, was an issue with her.

And all of this was going on whilst she knew if the surgery didn't go well she was looking at becoming a headline for all the wrong reasons.

Ecowarrior and Heartbroken Boring Daughter Found Dead in Mystery Shooting!

She shuddered as the true reality of the situation soaked through to her very core. Unless she helped save this man's life she and her father could lose theirs.

A tremor set light in her hands.

"Everything all right?" Diego's eyes snapped to hers, his instruments frozen in mid-air above Cruzito's entry wound.

"Sí. Muchas gracias."

Why was she speaking in her paltry Spanish? And why was she lying?

She forced herself to hold her hands steady, even though she was the opposite of all right. She was lurching from utter terror because— *hello!*—this was pretty terrifying and then slipping fleetingly into that beautiful, calm, quiet place that was medicine, where she knew she was in control.

She gave Diego another quick sidelong look and saw he was diligently back at work, completely unaware of her internal boxing match. If she could pull her right leg off and know she could trust him to ensure her father would be safe she would.

"I think it's best to leave the bullet in," Diego said without looking up.

"Why?"

She could have kicked herself for questioning him. This was *his* operating theatre. *His* set of rules. His scary gang of men, with an ominous overlord lurking out there somewhere, hopefully not torturing her father.

A thought struck. What if Diego was actually Axl Cruz? And this was *his* son?

Her mouth went completely dry.

Through the roar of blood in her head she could just hear Diego explaining his reasons why in that tobacco voice of his. Though she doubted he'd ever smoked so much as a cigarillo in his life. His personal aroma was more cocoa bean and coffee, with a splash of wood smoke just to ratchet up the alpha aura about him.

"Have you taken one out before?"

She shook her head and forced herself to answer in a steady, even voice. "Gunshot wounds are pretty rare in Loch Craggen. Handguns are illegal and hunting accidents are mercifully rare."

Diego made a throaty *humph* noise. She didn't need a translator to know what it meant. It meant, *Lucky you.*

A sliver of hope that he might actually be on the right side of the law flared inside her. Perhaps he was some sort of medical Robin Hood, stealing medical supplies to care for men who... Men who were holding her father captive.

Medicine. Just focus on the medicine.

"Any chance of lead poisoning?"

"No." He shook his head and asked her to hand him the hot blade used for cauterizing blood vessels. "Blood poisoning has largely been relegated to the past. These days leaving a bullet in is only a problem if the bullets are soaked in biological weapons. A double-edged sword."

He tipped his head to the side, then returned his focus to the web of open blood vessels.

"Thankfully, things are not that advanced here. There's more risk for Cruzito if we take it out. Further blood loss."

His eyes flicked to the solitary bag of O positive hanging on a stand.

"He was lucky nothing crucial was nicked apart from the lung. If it had been you know as well as I do that we wouldn't be standing here operating on him. This is all we have for now, so if something goes wrong it's better to let scar tissue grow round the bullet. Apart from problems going through airport security, the scar tissue around the bullet will protect the body from most complications. If not." His shoulders lifted in a casual shrug. "They know where I live."

A shiver of unease shuddered down her spine on his behalf. Although was he double-bluffing?

Before she could stop herself she asked, "Are you...one of them?"

His eyes pinged to hers and little crinkles fanned out from the edges as she saw the huff of a laugh inflate his face mask.

Was that a no? She didn't want it to be a yes.

Something deep in her gut told her it wasn't a yes. But it looked a whole lot more complicated than a simple no.

He didn't answer, instead continued to steadily cauterize blood vessels and clean out the wound.

She took the moment to steal another not so secret stare.

His jet-black lashes punctuated just how dark his irises were. She hadn't noticed they were flecked with gold before. Like dark spiced rum shot through with sunlight. Equal parts powerful and forgiving.

She saw his face mask move a bit. In, then out.

In the course of the boat ride she'd noticed Diego had a habit of shifting his tongue along his lower lip when he was concentrating. Then he'd pinch that same full lip between his teeth and slowly release it as his brows tucked together and those long fingers of his shifted through his hair.

All of which, she was horrified to discover, unleashed a heatwave of desire deep down in her most essential self. The easiest way to douse that fire was to remind herself that her life and her father's were very likely in his hands.

One tense and, mercifully successful hour of surgery later, Isla had finally willed her fingers into submission. No more shaking.

She took the clamps Diego handed her and put them on a sterilized tray. "You must be tired," she said. "Why don't you let me close…? What did you say his name was?"

"His nickname's Cruzito. Little Cruz," he translated. "His Christian name is Paz."

"That's an unusual name. Does it mean anything?"

Diego's eyes flicked to hers and cinched tight. "It means Peace."

Isla couldn't help herself. She laughed. "Seriously?"

Diego's shoulder lifted. "His *papà*'s name means Father of Peace."

"Axl Cruz? His first name means Father of Peace? He's got a funny way of showing it."

Diego tipped his head to the side, his dark eyes clouding for a minute before he looked at her and said, "Why don't you go on ahead and close up?"

Okay. She guessed she wasn't going to get any more answers on that front. The situation was far more complicated than bad guys wanting money and power.

Diego stood back from the table, pulled down his surgical mask and began clearing the area on his side of the surgical table without so much as a backward glance. The gesture felt…*huge*.

He didn't strike her as someone who freely handed over the reins at the surgical table. Nor did she think he would whimsically dole out trust and respect. He was a man who expected people to earn it.

And she liked earning it.

She dropped her gaze down to the black stubble on his throat, and just below it to where a thin leather strap hung round his neck. Whatever dangled at the end of it was weighting the leather below the V-neckline of his scrubs.

Her fingers twitched with the sudden urge to touch it. A whirl of self-loathing swept through her. She'd never had this sort of primal response to a man before. And he was her captor, no less.

As if she needed to feel even *more* vulnerable.

"Where is my father?"

"In time, *cariña*." His eyes met hers again, with that same unwavering strength.

Cariña? Seriously? The word, which she knew to be a term of endearment, felt discordant given the circumstances. He was in charge of the situation, as far as she could see. The only man apart from Axl Cruz the *pandilleros* would listen to. He was taller than most of them. Lean, but not skinny. Fit. He moved with leonine assurance. And a confidence that meant he knew his body could handle whatever he threw at it. A confidence that spoke of the power many surgeons held in their hands. The power to give and take life.

She tore her eyes from his and slowly, exactingly, began to close up the incisions with a combination of sutures and staples until Cruzito was ready to go into the small recovery room Diego had pointed out earlier. Two men were called in and they wheeled the lad away.

As they began cleaning the surgical tools a new man entered the room, with a couple of gunmen in his wake. He wasn't physically intimidating, in terms of height or musculature, but he radiated an aura of power. One that came from using fear as his main weapon. This had to be Axl Cruz.

He looked at the space where his son had been operated on, then rattled off a few staccato words to Diego.

"What is he saying?"

She would have gnawed her own arm off if it had made her fluent in Spanish. Particularly as *she* seemed to be the subject of the conversation.

The two men would say something, look at her as if they were sizing up a racehorse, then launch into a volley of speech again.

The gunmen looked utterly unmoved. As if this were an everyday sort of thing.

The only thing keeping her upright was the deep-seated need to be assured that her father was alive and well. That was it. Whatever it took to make that happen, she would do it.

When the rapid-fire conversation escalated,

then reached a crescendo, Diego slammed his fist down on a nearby table, causing all the instruments on it to jump. His entire demeanor spoke of a man who had given an ultimatum.

Isla swallowed.

Was he negotiating for *her*? For her freedom? There was no British Embassy or High Commission in El Valderon. She didn't even know an emergency number she could call for help. And even if she had she somehow knew that any such intervention would only throw more fuel onto a fire that was already raging out of control.

How strange that she felt as if Diego had her back on this. It wasn't something she was used to feeling. As if she were part of a team.

Her eyes pinged to Axl.

He gave a *whaddya want me to do about it?* shrug. He'd obviously given his ultimatum too. And it wasn't one that leant in her favor.

Axl turned and walked away, taking all the oxygen in the room with him.

Diego's hand moved to the leather strip around his neck as he asked the remaining gunman a question. It sounded like a taunt. Diego kept his eyes boring into the man, until he too shrugged and left the room.

Isla watched, transfixed, as Diego curled his right index finger round the leather thong and, with one swift tug, freed the leather strap from his neck.

"Take off your gloves."

"What?"

She shook her head, not understanding, but did it anyway. Heat surged from her fingers up her arm and swirled round her collarbone as he took her left hand in his. She felt something cool slipped on to her finger.

What she saw drew all the breath from her lungs.

A ring. A beautiful triumvirate of gold, silver and platinum bands linked together. At the apex, nestled amongst the bands, was one of the largest diamonds she had ever seen.

"What on—?" Confusion drowned out her ability to think straight. She looked up and met his solid gaze. "What is this for?"

"Marry me."

Diego was as shocked to hear himself ask Isla to marry him as she looked to receive a proposal.

When she remained drop-jawed, he said it again. "Marry me, Isla."

His voice sounded alien to him. Thick with emotion. Urgent. Not conveying the usual cool demeanor he'd worn as armor since his heart had all but been torn from his chest.

Desperate times. Desperate measures.

Isla shook her head, as if it would alter the words she'd just heard. "I'm sorry. Does that mean the same thing here as it means in Scotland? Because where I come from it means become husband and wife."

"I'm pretty sure I've proved my fluency in English." He felt his features harden. A muscle twitch in his jaw. The opposite of what one would expect from a lovestruck groom. A narky comment and a thunder face.

Muchas gracias, Noche Blanca. Once again you've managed to bring out my better side.

"I don't understand."

How could she? She lived in a kinder world. One where survival wasn't an issue. One where a marriage proposal didn't sit at the polar extreme of *Romance 101.*

"Marry me. To save your father. To save yourself."

Axl had been crystal-clear. The only way he would back off from the sanctuary was if Doug MacLeay was out of the picture. Permanently.

Diego could only think of one way to save Doug and Isla's lives. An old vow on top of a new one.

After his brother's death, Axl had promised safety for every member of his family. And there was only one way to make Doug and Isla part of his family. So he told Axl he was in love with

Isla. A whirlwind romance neither of them could fight.

Axl's response had been immediate. "You say you love this woman? Fine. Be my guest. Marry her. *Tonight*."

Otherwise…?

This was where the infamous Axl Cruz shrug had come in. Otherwise they would both go. And not back to Scotland.

It was that simple.

So here he was standing in front of a woman he didn't know, praying she would agree to marry him.

A door banged in the distance, followed by a loud volley of men's voices.

"This is ridiculous. Surely now that Cruzito is all right they'll let us go?"

Diego shook his head. "No. It doesn't work that way. You've both seen too much. Caused too much trouble."

"Trouble? Are you kidding—?"

He held a finger to her lips, wondering if she felt the same heat he felt pouring through his hand. If it was searing straight through to *her* tongue, *her* throat. What was it about this woman that was making him behave like this?

He dropped his hand and crushed his physiological response.

"They will kill your father. No question.

You…?" He held his palms up. "You helped save his son's life. That might count for something."

For a millisecond he saw fear ripple across her features. An instant later it was gone. He recognized the same mask he so often donned. The one he wore when he told patients they had cancer. Told parents that their child had an incurable illness. The one he'd worn ever since his own brother had died saving the son of the criminal who all but held their island hostage.

She nodded that she understood.

"Put on a pair of fresh gloves," Diego instructed.

Insane or not, it was a plan that might work. Why or how he'd chosen this woman, this moment, to pull in a favor he would never have again was a question he couldn't ask himself right now. Axl could sniff weakness and lies as easily as you could smell the salt in the air.

"We have to convince him this is what we want. That we met when you first arrived and that we're already engaged."

"But I only arrived a few days ago!"

"Never heard of love at first sight?"

She flushed and looked away.

Did she…? Had she felt it too? That crackle of connection?

Don't be an idiot. It wasn't love. It was lust.

He believed in lust. Passion, even. But love?

He didn't believe in love anymore. Couldn't. Not when he knew how the world really worked.

"When the men come back in again take the gloves off. They won't know they're a different pair. Make sure the diamond hits the light. They need to see the ring."

Isla pursed her lips, looked at her hand, then nodded, tendrils of auburn hair masking her expression. He pulled his fingers into a fist, willing them not to tease a few of those wayward curls into submission. This wasn't the time to go all *Romeo and Juliet* on her.

She sniffed and shook her hair back, as if she was annoyed at his choice of paint for their new living room rather than being thrown into a vortex of fear and confusion. Most people would have been annoyed if their lives depended upon marrying a complete stranger.

"Do you always carry engagement rings around your neck? Just in case?"

She met his gaze straight on, defiance crackling through her blue eyes where he'd convinced himself he'd see gratitude.

She began tugging it off of her finger. "I've got an idea. Why don't you take this ring and let me have a phone so I can ring the police? I'd prefer *that* type of ring."

He almost laughed. Isla's hair wasn't the only thing made of fire.

Being forced to marry someone against your will was not ideal. Even so... He genuinely couldn't see another way round this.

He took the ring and slid it back on to her finger. "The walls have ears, *amorcita*. Best to keep your voice low."

"Why can't we call the police?"

She pressed her lips together until they drained of blood, glaring at him until he explained.

"The police won't intervene. They let matters of this variety sort themselves out." Just as they'd refused an escort for the ambulance that might have saved his brother's life.

"What on earth does that mean?"

"Too many pockets are lined with ill-gained gold."

"Are you kidding me?"

It keeps their families safe.

Diego's gaze flicked to the door, then back to Isla. "The ring. It's my grandmother's. I have never put it on anyone's finger. Never wanted to."

He let the words settle between them, but the intensity of his delivery meant they might as well have been shot directly from the center of his heart.

It shocked him to realize how genuine his sentiments were. Did he *love* her? Of course not. Would he take a sacred vow to care and protect her? Without a doubt.

Why her? Why now?

He smashed the thoughts back into his Questions to Remain Unanswered cupboard and kicked the door shut.

"I need a reason to believe you," she said. "Just one."

"Your life is at risk. Your father's life." And he couldn't let what happened to his brother happen to another family.

Isla's blue eyes glassed over, then cleared. She pulled on a fresh pair of gloves, and both of them were glued to the sight of the sparkling diamond disappearing beneath the light blue Neoprene.

A man walked in. He looked tired. Disheveled. As if he was there under duress.

Isla's eyes widened as she took in the man's dog collar.

Trust Noche Blanca to rustle up a priest in the dead of night, thought Diego.

The black thought that he might have been brought in earlier to deliver the last rites to Isla and her father crossed his mind. He slashed the thought in two, reminding himself that the poor man was more likely to be there to do the same for Cruzito.

His expression told Diego the last thing he thought he'd be performing was a wedding ceremony.

A grim smile teased at the corners of Diego's

mouth. This was Axl putting him to the test. The "big doctor man" claimed to be in love with this woman? Well, there was only one way to prove it as far as Axl Cruz was concerned. Follow his lead. He'd met and married his own wife in a whirlwind twenty-four-hour romance. So Diego would do the same.

"Why is he forcing us to do this *now*? In the middle of the night?"

"It's a test."

He heard the emotion in his chest transforming his voice into something he'd never heard come from his own throat. Low, gravelly. Urgent.

"He promised long ago never to hurt my family. If you want to get out of this unharmed we must marry. I told him you were my fiancée. That we met when you first got here and fell in love in an instant. That I couldn't imagine my life without you."

Isla clenched the edge of the table with both hands. Was there a glimmer in her eyes? Just a hint of wanting what he said to be true?

¡Ni en sueños!

He was reading into things. Turning this into something it very distinctly wasn't. If he let himself go down that path none of them would survive.

Caring, loving, mourning—allowing himself to feel that triumvirate of powerful emotions had got him where he was today. Trapped by his own vow always to serve. No matter what the circumstances.

None of it would bring his brother back. But doing this one thing might ease the pain.

He looked into Isla's eyes, drilling it into his brain that doing this was purely to save the Professor and his daughter. Nothing more. No matter what the blood careening round his veins was suggesting.

Diego reached across and cupped Isla's face in his hand as a lover would. "If you want to save your father you will follow my lead."

She shook her head. Whether it was a no or a response to his touch was unclear. He pulled her closer—not to control her, but to hide the panic in her eyes from the guards as they darted about the room.

This house, a mishmash of surgery and hideaway, was hardly a dream destination for a wedding day.

He could easily picture Isla wanting something informal on the beach. A simple dress. Bare shoulders, perhaps. Some flowers in her hair. A look of pure and unfettered love in her eyes…

An insane urge to promise her something else, something better once they got through this, launched into his throat, barely giving him time to bite it back.

The gunman and the priest were openly waiting for Isla to make a move. She had seconds, if that, to decide.

Isla closed her eyes as Diego ran his hand down her neck and cupped it, moving his other hand to the base of her throat, resting his thumbs on her collarbones. She knew what he was doing. Playing a role. An insane role to see through an insane plan. But at this juncture did she have any other choice?

Her eyes flickered open as he whispered her name. When she connected to his rock-solid gaze one last time he said, "Do this. Marry me."

His touch, the intimacy, the intensity of his request—it should have felt threatening. Terrifying, even. Astonishingly, from Diego, it felt more... *protective*. Caring...

It was a gesture that, if seen by someone who didn't know them, would have made the onlooker think she and Diego had known one another for years. Had been lovers, even. The way she naturally leaned into his caresses made it appear even more so. Little would they know it was terror at her father's imprisonment compelling her to believe Diego. Believe there was a way out of this mess.

Can you do this? Marry this stranger?

Axl appeared in the doorway and began speaking to Diego in a low voice.

Diego held up a hand. *"Momentito, por favor, Axl."*

The temperature in the room seemed to drop as Axl held his ground.

She caught his eye as he turned to leave the room. He looked at her and smiled, but there was no warmth in it.

"You're a lucky woman." He tipped his head toward Diego. "This is the only man on this island that I trust as one of my own."

Isla was about to say her father was every bit as trustworthy as Diego, but felt Diego's fingers press into her shoulder.

Axl turned and left the room.

"Isla." Diego spoke urgently now. "Listen to me. *Marry me*. It's the only way to save your father's life."

Glacier water shot through her veins. For the first time since the gunmen had shown up at the sanctuary Isla felt genuine fear. And that was saying something.

All that had seemed surreal—dreamlike, even—now hardened into ice-cold reality.

She had to do it.

"Your father's work is very important, but these men are…they're *tricky* to negotiate with."

No kidding. People who wielded guns and threatened to kill folk often were.

She pulled back, her spine braced as new fear struck. "Will it be…? Will it be a *real* marriage?"

Diego's full lips thinned. His expression spoke volumes. He wasn't the sort of man to take advantage of a woman. "It's a means to an end. You need protection. If you marry me you will be family—just as your father will be."

"You'll be lucky." She spat the words more out of fear than venom.

Much to her surprise, Diego nodded. "Yes," he said. "Yes, I will be. You may need to stay here awhile, but if we go ahead with this now we can negotiate your father's release. Get him on a plane back to Scotland. Safe."

The words were a salve to her raw emotions. Even so… "How long is 'awhile'?"

He shrugged as if time meant nothing. In these circumstances she supposed it didn't. "Marriage is something they take seriously here. You must stay with me for at least one month before—"

"*One month?* Why?" The logistics of staying away that long crashed into her solid, practical side.

"It's the end of the mating season. For the sea turtles," he qualified.

As if he needed to. It wasn't as if he and she

were going to be doing any mating during this… this sham marriage.

"I—" She stopped herself.

One month. It would save her father's life.

She swallowed the lump in her throat. She would stay forever if it meant her father could live the rest of his life without fear of harm.

"Fine. A month." She wanted to quibble. Say it sounded to her like he was making things up on the fly. She said it again so he knew she meant it.

He continued to explain, masking their chat in that low, rumbling voice of his that might just as easily be lavishing her with compliments.

"In public we must be seen as man and wife. In my home—our home—" he corrected "—we will work out the particulars of how it will work."

"The marriage?"

"*Sí, mi amor*. The marriage."

She knew enough Spanish to know he was using another term of endearment. Was he coercing her or comforting her?

She sought answers in those dark eyes of his and found solace in them. Honesty. He wouldn't hurt her. She would be safe.

This was definitely something she would never be able to encapsulate on the postcard she'd promised to send Dougray Campbell, whose blood pressure she'd finally got under control. Not that any of this was doing much for hers.

She could hear the blood roaring around her head, her heart, but when she blinked and re-aligned her focus on Diego's dark brown eyes she felt safe again.

What had happened to him to make him sacrifice his own future this way? If these men were as violent as they seemed and he had one favor why was he using it for her?

It wasn't for *her*. She was a means to the end. Saving her father was the goal. He was promising peace and economic stability for the island. To a man who clearly loved his home and his profession, a prosperous, peaceful nation would surely be the answer to a thousand prayers.

When the priest cleared his throat Diego gave him a quick nod, then put his entire focus on Isla. "I know nothing about this is normal. I know you must be scared." He looked her straight in the eye. "But you can trust me. We can work out how we approach things later. How we untangle the net. But if you want to save your father we must do this. We must marry. Now."

"*Now*—now?"

The priest stepped toward them.

Well, that answered that, then.

At least her long engagement to Kyle had meant she'd been dropped before the wedding bells chimed.

A mad thought flew into her head.

Had fate thrown her into Diego's arms? Had things fallen to bits back in Loch Craggen because she was meant to be *here*?

One month…

A month she already knew was going to change her life forever.

She heard the clank of a gun against the doorframe as one of the Noche Blanca members entered the room.

Violence had thrown them together. Violence that wouldn't end if she didn't agree to this harebrained scheme. This *life-saving* scheme.

Isla's brain was reeling so fast she felt dizzy.

Her father was the kindest, most gentle man she'd ever known. After her mother had died his compassion had doubled instead of evaporating. Not many men who'd lost a wife to senseless violence would have found it in their hearts to see her dreams through.

You might have thought a quiet life with his daughter, researching otters in the farther reaches of Scotland, might be enough for him. But, no. His passion to carry on with his wife's work with endangered species had become his lifeblood.

Isla knew more than anyone that her father would be the last one to save himself if it meant compromising an endangered species. Science and nature spoke to him more loudly than common sense. More loudly than his love for his child.

In her case blood was thicker than water. She was going to have to agree to this hare-brained plan.

At least she wasn't required to fall in love with him.

Say yes. Save yourself. Save your father. Figure out how to get out of it later.

What if you don't want to?

"How can I be sure they'll let my father go back to Scotland? Safely?"

Diego dropped his hands to his sides. She watched his fingers stretch, then curl into fists as he answered. "He gave his word."

She couldn't help it. She laughed. "So you're saying if I agree to marry you—bearing in mind they've been aiming guns at me and my father all night—they will let my father go back to Scotland unharmed?"

Diego nodded, not a trace of humor lighting up those eyes of his.

Something else was. Something indecipherable.

Pain? Loss?

"And if he refuses to go?"

"For now? He must. Until the end of the egg-laying season. It is the only way or they *will* kill him."

That answered that, then. "How do I know they won't kill me once my father's on the plane?"

"They won't." His voice was solid. He didn't blink.

"Why should I believe anything they say?"

He tilted his head to the side, eyes still glued to hers. It was a gesture that said a thousand things at once—including the one that counted the most.

You can trust me.

"When Noche Blanca make a deal, they honor it." He turned and shifted his gaze to the doorway, where a pair of men in black clothes were wheeling the gurney with Cruzito on it into yet another room where his father was waiting. "They owe me."

It was all she needed to hear.

"Fine," she said. "I'll do it."

CHAPTER FOUR

"Sí, QUIERO." DIEGO now understood the phrase "going through the motions." Hardly what he had imagined his wedding day would be like. Not that he'd imagined it. *Ever.* Going through years of relentless family tragedy had a way of casting a pall over the idea of marital bliss.

He nodded to the priest.

So this was it. He was halfway to becoming a married man. There'd be some hoops to jump through to get…unembroiled…but it wasn't as if life hadn't prepared him for a bit of elasticity when it came to survival.

That was how it worked on El Valderon. You picked a system and went with it. Above the law. Within the law. Or his way. Skirting the perimeters of everything to help those who needed medical care. It was that simple.

There'd be peace one day. Justice. But for now…? He was strangely looking forward to a few weeks of seeing the world through the eyes of his fiery-haired wife. A woman who looked about as thrilled to marry him as Axl had looked when he'd agreed to let Isla's father travel back to Scotland with a guarantee of safety. A *lifelong* guarantee. It had come with the condition he'd presumed it would. Isla must stay here, with her *esposo*.

In just a few moments she would be Isla Vasquez.

Funny… He liked the sound of it. Being part of a team. Doing things on his own had its benefits, but to have someone by his side…

Alto! This was an arrangement. Not a love match.

Diego spun his finger round in a *speed things up* gesture—which the priest ignored. He seemed keen on fleshing out the ceremony. The man wasn't oblivious to what was happening. It was the middle of the night and gunmen were aiming their weapons at the happy couple. Foolishly, the poor man was giving her a chance to back out.

Isla stared at the priest, her lower lip clamped so tightly beneath her teeth Diego wouldn't be surprised if she soon drew blood.

He was tempted to lean down and kiss her. Just to give that lip some relief.

Dios. That was an excuse. He *wanted* to kiss the bride. *His* bride.

The doctor in him knew that adrenaline and testosterone were overriding common sense. It was why men could roar into battle. Fear masked as courage fueled by the body's biological will to survive.

He watched Isla as her brow furrowed and her eyes narrowed as she tried to understand the priest's extensive preamble to the very simple question *Will you marry Diego Vasquez?*

A blast of heat lit up areas he hadn't thought about in the same context as marriage. One-night stands. A handful of friendships with benefits. Those had kept him running through the years. And they would carry on doing so after Isla was safely back home—because, he reminded himself, none of this was real.

"¿Quiere a Diego Vasquez por esposo?" The priest gave Isla an expectant look.

Diego squeezed her hand and gave her a soft smile. "At this point you're meant to say, *Sí, quiero.*"

"I am not going to say anything I don't understand," she snapped.

Where he would have expected to feel a flare of irritation at the fact that Isla wasn't just going along with things, he felt his heart soften with compassion. Fair enough. This was being done under duress. In a foreign language. Most people would have tears pouring down their face now.

Not Isla. He could see her battling her fear into submission—and winning. But if she wanted to

save her life and, her father's, she'd be wise to
follow his cues.

This was foreign territory for him as well. He
wasn't a "save the damsel in distress" sort of
guy. Not that Isla seemed weak. But she did need
help. *His* help.

"How about I translate?"

She gave him a nod. One that said, *I'm not
happy about this, but I'll do anything to save my
father.* His heart twisted tight at the shot of fear
that flashed through her eyes. Twisted once more
when he saw it turn to anguish.

He brushed the back of his hand against her
soft, pale cheek and against the odds she leaned
into it. The intimacy of the moment suddenly
made the vows they were mid-way through ex-
changing feel that much more real. They were in
this together. He wasn't the white knight riding
in and saving her. They were playing equal roles
in a dangerous game of survival.

"He's asked if you will accept me as your husband. I have already accepted you as my wife.
So now you say, *Si, quiero.* It means you accept."

For an instant he thought her veneer of strength
was going to crack. In the next he saw her entire
body fill with resolve. Determination. It was an
extraordinary thing to witness. The power of fa-
milial love. It made him proud to have made the

decision he had. The first hit of genuine pride he'd felt since Nico had died.

"*Sí.*" She gave his hand a squeeze as she confirmed. "*Sí, quiero.*"

The priest pronounced them man and wife, and before another moment passed Diego gave in to impulse, put his hands on Isla's waist, pulled her to him and kissed her.

He would have loved to say he was gentle. He would've loved to say that the very first time their lips met it was with the softest touch his reluctant wife had ever known.

But the emotion heating up his veins was the past colliding with the present. When his mouth reached hers there was hunger in his touch. And fire.

The next few hours were frantic with activity. So much so that Isla periodically forgot to be blindsided by the fact that she was now, in the eyes of the Catholic church and the El Valderon government, Señora Isla Vasquez.

The whole thing was so ludicrous it was impossible to register. In just a few short days she'd gone from being engaged, to dumped, to married.

She was a wife.

In name only. Obviously.

But…

Her fingers drifted up to her lips and traced

them as if that would turn back time. What she couldn't forget was that kiss. She'd never in her life felt anything like the lightning strike of connection she'd felt when Diego had kissed her. It hadn't been an ordinary kiss. Not like anything she'd experienced before. He had been tasting her. Exploring her. *Possessing her.*

She pressed her eyes tight and an image of him instantly pinged to the fore.

Tall. Caramel-skinned. Mahogany eyes flecked with gold. Long fingers. Strong arms. A body that filled out clothes in a way only a man who possessed leonine grace could.

And an above par surgeon.

The man who had saved three lives in one night.

Paz's. Her father's. And her own.

Diego was the stuff of fairy tales.

The kind that didn't always end so well for the Princess, she curtly reminded herself. There was a reason those stories didn't venture beyond the wedding.

She held up yet another book to her father. "Staying or going?"

"That one *has* to come back to Loch Craggen with me."

She gave her father an exasperated smile. "Dad. You can't take them all. We've got to get to the airport in less than an hour and there's usually some sort of weight restriction."

As if following the rules mattered anymore.

Her mind pinged to her pathetic carry-on bag with its two skirts and two T-shirts. One of each was ruined now. And she was still wearing the scrubs Diego had given her.

Her shoulders shifted along the fabric. She was too aware of the broad shoulders that would normally fill them. Though he was her husband now, there was a part of her that wanted to claw them off. To demand that for once she be allowed to be her own woman.

Not the rule-follower. Not the good daughter. Not the pragmatic GP. A woman who made her own decisions. Chose her own path. Wasn't forced to marry a man at gunpoint because her father valued turtles over his daughter.

"There won't be a weight restriction on business class."

"Business class?"

"Your husband's way of making the transition less painful, I suppose." He returned her perplexed smile with a weary one of his own. "You picked a good one, you know."

"What?" *What on earth was he on about?*

"Diego," her father explained unnecessarily. "He will be a good husband for you."

"Father!" Her nerves crackled with a peculiar mix of indignation and something else. Hope?

She tsked away the thought. "I married Diego so that Noche Blanca wouldn't *kill* us. Don't you remember that part?"

Her father tipped his head from side to side, as if wedlock under duress might not have been the only option available to her.

Was he stark raving mad?

The little girl in her wanted to throw herself on the floor and have a proper tantrum. Couldn't he see what his actions had done? It was her mother all over again. Wading into the danger zone with no thought for the family she'd leave behind.

"Anyway…" She primly packed the rest of the books into the box without bothering to ask. "It's only for a month."

"That's what he told you?"

Isla's heart-rate careened into a sprint. "Do you think he was lying?"

Her father feigned interest in a book he was about to put into the box. "Island time works differently. So does Diego Vasquez."

Isla was about to ask what on earth that meant when, as if on cue, Diego poked his head through the open front door of the small bungalow her father had been staying in. Then he looked back over his shoulder when someone called his name.

Her pounding heart launched into her throat

and her fingers automatically flew to her lips, as if seeing him brought back each and every moment of that searing kiss. It was as if they'd been branded into her cell structure. *In a good way.*

She scraped her nails along her lips, begging the accompanying pain to tear the memory from her.

Diego entered the room and he and her father quietly discussed logistics as she tried to attach reason to her physical response to her husband. Fear and excitement often felt the same. It was why people loved watching horror films. The thrill of surviving something terrifying. A physiological response to something outside of your control.

How else could she explain the powerful connection she'd felt when their lips had not only touched, but had sought each other as if their lives depended on it.

Hers had.

His hadn't.

And yet…

She looked at him, filling the doorway in a non-threatening way. Protectively. It wasn't the body language she'd experienced when he'd pulled her to him after they had been pronounced man and wife. His kiss had had intent. His hands on her body had had the feel of a man claiming something. As if he'd finally claimed her after a hard-fought battle to win her heart. As if he loved her with every fiber of his being.

But when she'd pushed at his chest he'd let go of her as if she'd been made of fire.

Would you have pushed away or pulled closer if you'd married Kyle?

Was this the point when she would admit to herself that she'd always known they weren't meant for one another? That someone else was out there?

"You two are ready?" Diego waited a moment, then gave the doorframe a one-two pat, as if their lack of response was all the answer he needed. "*Ahora.* I'll be driving you, but don't be alarmed if there appear to be...escorts."

"Axl?" Her father gave his head a distracted shake, as if this were all perfectly normal.

The two of them began discussing a route to the airport that would draw the least attention.

"I want people to know the sanctuary is still that. A sanctuary." Her father met Diego's gaze and said solidly, "And I'm not just talking about the turtles."

It struck Isla that maybe this was her father's way of dealing with her mother's death. Providing sanctuary to anything and everything he could. Even if it came at the cost of his own safety.

He was a scientist. One who understood the

"risk" part of "risk assessment" much more than most. She should too, with her medical background. Operations weren't always successful. A small fever could kill. One day—any day—a person's heart could just stop.

Science didn't make up for loss, though. Not in her book. The day her mother had been killed was the day she had become an "i" dotter and a "t" crosser. The one who was *there*. The one who could be counted on. The one who would marry a stranger so her father could live to save another living being that wasn't his daughter.

Diego shifted and turned in the doorframe as a man approached the bungalow.

Something stirred in her that took the edge off the waves of fear. *Gratitude.* She owed her life to this man Dr. Diego Vasquez. A total stranger to her yesterday, and today he was her husband. Her *esposo.* It was plain as the nose on her face that he was no ordinary man. Not here on El Valderon, anyway.

She checked herself. *Not anywhere.*

He seemed to wield some sort of invisible power over the islanders. Not the power of force. Or of cruelty. The power of...*vision.* A man who left change in his wake. A man who had the power to convince her father he needed to leave his project if he had any hope of it ever succeeding.

Little short of a miracle in her book.

"Isla?"

Her heart squeezed tight as she looked at her dad. She didn't want him to leave.

"What do you think if I miss the flight?"

But she did want him to *live*.

"No, Dad. Absolutely not. You are getting on that plane." It was role reversal of the strangest kind. The child parenting the parent.

They talked back and forth in hurried whispers as Diego continued to talk to the man on the patio.

"What good are you to the turtles if you're dead?"

That was her final argument. The one that eventually convinced him to unearth his long-legged trousers. His hiking boots. Woolen socks. The worn green backpack he'd taken with him near enough everywhere in the world apart from home to Loch Craggen.

"The key to the house is at the surgery. My locum is called Dr. McCracken. There's not much to know about the house, but don't be surprised if Miss Laird nips in to water the plants. I've not been able to get hold of her yet to tell her you're on your way home."

"Miss Laird?"

Her father had no memory for names. Especially for the women of Craggen. There'd been only one woman for him, as he'd said on the rare occasions when he let himself revisit the past, *"and she's gone now."*

"She has been on the island about four years now. You'll like her. Mary Laird," Isla continued, "She has a small animal rescue shelter near the surgery—dogs, mostly, I think, but she'll take on anything. Last I heard she was nursing a seal. She sometimes does reception shifts for us at the surgery."

Her father barely seemed to register the information and she didn't blame him. If his thoughts were pinging round from topic to topic like hers were his brain was mush.

When they'd put the last book that would fit into his pack and sealed it, they stood and faced one another. He looked more weary than she had ever seen him. At fifty-eight he was hardly old, but the fine lines she'd seen round his eyes were now creases. And the gray at his temples had shot through the rest of his dark hair, giving him more salt than pepper. It hadn't happened overnight, of course. But it felt like it. His exhaustion had been accrued over years, but she felt as though it was the very first time she'd actually seen how much his diligent work had aged him.

The lines, the gray hair, the slightly hunched shoulders… She now realized they weren't just from fatigue. This was what defeat looked like.

MacLeays weren't very good at admitting defeat. Maybe that was one of the reasons why she'd turned a blind eye to all the glaring problems in her relationship with Kyle? The varied interests. His late nights to her early mornings. His crumpets and jam to her plain toast with butter.

"What do you want me to tell folk back home?"

Her heart thumped against her rib cage for a whole new reason. It was the first time her father had called Loch Craggen "home" in years. If ever.

"What do you think we should say?"

"Oh…" He pressed a couple of tentative fingers to his eye, which was quickly turning black.

He'd told her he had fallen against a chair when he was "chatting away" with the Cruz family. She believed that about as much as she believed Diego Vasquez was in love with her.

"I think I'll tell them I had a bit of regrouping to do and that you agreed to stay on to look after things at the sanctuary. You will, won't you?"

She nodded. The run-in with Noche Blanca had scared him. It made her blood boil. Made her want to stay and see her father's vision through to its fruition. Bring peace to the island and longevity to the welfare of the sea turtle.

Piece of cake.

Right?

She forced a plucky smile so that her father

couldn't see that her insides were turning into liquid fear.

"I'll come back." He pulled her into his arms. "And not just for the turtles," he whispered into her hair. "I'll come back for you."

Her heart nearly exploded with a combination of grief and love. How she wanted to believe it was true.

For the first time in her life she had absolutely no idea what her future looked like. She'd spent nearly every school holiday with her grandmother, because her father, once again, had forgotten to collect her from boarding school. She loved the man to within an inch of her life. He was her father. But he wasn't so great at keeping promises.

Maybe that was why she'd said yes to Kyle's proposal. Hoping against hope that she might be enough for an obvious playboy to change his ways.

Served her right for trying to change a man. The only person she could change was herself.

Diego, who she was quickly realizing seemed to have a sort of sixth sense of when he'd be needed, appeared in the doorway again. "Everything all right, *corazón*?"

He lifted her father's book-heavy backpack to the car as the two of them followed behind, each carrying a box.

Diego drove them to the airport in an open-topped Jeep. As predicted, there were a couple of ominous SUVs with tinted windows following behind. The Noche Blanca crew were ensuring that Professor MacLeay not only got on a plane but on the right one, with only a one-way ticket to his name.

As she waved goodbye to her father, after one last hug, then watched him disappear beyond the security gates it shocked her to realize her gut instinct was to turn to Diego for comfort.

Diego reached across from the driver's side of his car, only just stopping himself from giving Isla's leg a light squeeze. Again and again he found himself reaching out to touch her, comfort her. Again and again he reminded himself he was not the marrying kind. He'd never wanted to be a husband or a father. Even so…he didn't like seeing her face look so drawn.

"He'll be safe now."

Isla nodded and wove her fingers tightly together, watching as the blood drained from them. She drew a sharp breath, as if to launch into a speech about how loathsome she found this entire situation, then reconsidered, and, after steadying her breath said simply, "Thank you."

The words were so heartfelt they sucker-punched him straight in the chest.

He reminded himself that her gratitude was solely for her father's welfare. Not for any heroics on his part. Or kissing. Or marriage. Or any of it. She would have done anything to save her father. Just as he would have to save his brother, if he hadn't been away at medical school.

"Of course."

"What's that old saying?" she asked.

Isla drummed her fingers along her lips. Lips he would resist kissing again if he had to drain the very marrow from his bones. Isla MacLeay was not his to love.

"Marry at haste and repent at leisure?"

He gave his thick stubble a scrub. "That sounds about right."

She gave her shoulders a shake and let out a huff of air. No doubt psyching herself into her new reality.

"Well!" She unwove her fingers, rubbed her hands together, then let them land in her lap with a clap so sharp he knew it must have stung. "I guess that gives us a month of leisure," she said, without a trace of joy.

He was about to correct her. Say he wasn't sure about the timing. He'd just been making a stab in the dark last night. Working with men who circumnavigated the law as if it were lethal nerve gas took care. Delicacy.

"To us and our month of leisure!"

Without a thought, he took her hand in his, drew it to his lips and kissed the back of it. It was a strangely natural thing to do. Just as it had been when he'd pulled her into his arms after her father had disappeared into the departure lounge, and then again when they'd watched his plane rise and soar off into the deep blue sky.

Though her eyes were hidden by huge movie star sunglasses, and he'd not seen her shed a single tear, he had little doubt there'd be shadows beneath them.

"You must be exhausted."

She looked down at their hands as if they were foreign objects, then tipped her head back against the headrest, letting the wind ripple through that amazing hair of hers. Lit, as it was, by the late-morning sun, it was flame-colored.

"You're right. It would be fair to say I could probably do with a wee bit of a lie-down."

"Not long now."

She pulled off her sunglasses and crinkled her brow in that endearing way of hers.

He looked away.

This is for show only. When she's safe you'll let her go. Just as you let everything in your life go.

"I thought your place was down past the sanctuary." She pointed in the opposite direction. "We only drove a few minutes to get to your surgery."

"That's my…" He sought his English vocabulary for the most neutral description. "That's a facility Axl kindly accepted on behalf of the community."

Diego had donated the land and bungalow after his brother had taken a bullet for Axl's eldest son. Axl owed him favors, all right. Favors that would never be paid in full.

"Axl Cruz? The leader of *Noche Blanca*?"

"That's right."

"He doesn't strike me as a community-minded sort of man. Unless…" The lightbulb went on. "The clinic is only open to members of Noche Blanca."

No getting anything past her.

He thought of the scores of knife wounds he'd stitched up there. The bullets he'd extracted. The children of men who had grown up alongside his own father who had lain on that very same table Axl's son had been on this morning. There wasn't a chance in hell he'd live in that place. Not with the ghosts it housed.

"Suffice it to say it is a convenience they are willing to pay for."

"A convenience that ensures anyone in Noche Blanca who is injured while they are committing a crime receives treatment?"

"*Si*. The island hospital isn't staffed well enough to treat everyone who needs it. And more often than not the people involved in those sorts of activities are nervous about going to the hospital, where they would risk arrest."

"Can anyone else use it? The farmers who live nearby? It must be convenient for them as the hospital is on the far side of the island."

"No. It is for Noche Blanca only."

"What if the victims aren't gang members? Would an ambulance come for them? One from the hospital?"

"Not if they have anything to do with members of Noche Blanca. Family, friends…any kind of connection."

Saying that out loud never failed to bring a twist of bile into his throat. He waited for it to pass. "How do you mean? A patient's a patient where I come from."

"Music to my ears, *cariña*."

He meant it, too. It was his credo. A patient was a patient.

He cleared his throat and spoke as if by rote. "Here on El Valderon resources are extremely limited. The island has never had a very settled democracy since it was liberated from its colonial past, and suffice it to say not losing their ambulance staff to Noche Blanca is a priority."

"Is that a nice way of saying the baddies beat the goodies?"

"No. Not so simple."

He ran his fingers along the edges of his steering wheel to stop himself reaching out to her again. Touching her was hardly a way to remind himself that the marriage was a fake. *Facts.* Just stick to the facts and the month would soon be over. Then he could get back to his one-man crusade to slowly restore balance on the island.

"Axl is one of many men who took advantage of the poor in a handful of newly independent countries here in the Caribbean. Many people—laborers, mostly—who thought they might finally get some financial traction are still poor. Axl and his kind took advantage of them, telling them they deserved to be a part of being rich. That they shouldn't let the few who became very wealthy without sweating for it stay that way."

He swallowed back the bit of family history he wasn't particularly proud of. Isla would find out soon enough that he was one of the privileged few.

"How did the wealthy get that way?"

"Sugar is a big crop here. Tourism would make more money—*much* more—if the island's reputation for crime could be beaten. Not literally, of course," he added with a wicked grin.

He'd forced himself to keep his sense of humor over the years. Even if it did lurch into darker realms from time to time.

"So why steal the turtle eggs if they know that eco-tourism would help?"

"Have you ever cried yourself to sleep because you were hungry?"

She shook her head.

"A lot of people here have."

"And the government doesn't help?"

"It does what it can. But with so few people able to pay taxes it takes its toll. On the police force, the municipal services, the hospital."

He'd do more—work round the clock if he could—but he was drawn again and again to his work "behind the scenes." Trying, day by day, to pay penance for not being there for his brother.

"Why don't you work at the hospital full-time? Wouldn't that help with the staffing problems?"

"I already do."

He left it at that. No need to pour out his family history in one fell swoop.

She kept her eyes on the coastal road they were traveling and quietly asked, "What about *your* family? How did this journey toward democracy work for the Vasquez family?"

"You're one of us now, *mija*. Don't forget you'll be painted with the same brush."

She bristled. "Then I guess you'd better answer the question. Where does your family stand in El Valderon?

"Depends upon who you ask."

She sucked in a sharp breath. "*Ay, papi!* That sounds mysterious."

As dark as he'd felt the moment before, light filled him, like the sun coming out from behind a dark cloud. He laughed a full belly laugh, sweeping some hair away from Isla's face only to discover her cheeks flushed an adorable hot pink.

"Where did you learn that?"

"What?" She looked utterly mortified.

"That saying. *Ay, papi!* Where did you learn that?"

She pressed her hands between her knees and scrunched up her lips as she tried to remember. *Damn.* That was adorable, too.

"Television?" She sounded embarrassed to admit it. Then grew indignant. "It's what you say when you're admonishing someone, isn't it? Like, *Come on, you obfuscator! Tell me the truth!*"

He tried, unsuccessfully, to disguise his second hit of hysterics as a cough. "No. That's not what it means. It's a turn of phrase you should save for…"

He scrubbed his hand through his hair. *Did he really want to go there?*

"Save it for what?"

She looked genuinely interested.

Dios. He scrubbed his jaw, his mouth, trying to wipe off the smile.

"It's something you might say if we were in our early twenties." *And naked. In bed.*

"Thirty-one doesn't exactly make me geriatric." She gave him a blue-eyed *Don't pigeonhole me, matey* glare and shrug, clearly waiting for a better explanation.

How did he explain that if she were ever to say it—which he doubted—she'd be more likely to *scream* it. Howl it or growl it. Moan it out of sheer rapture when both their bodies were bathed in sweat, his hands on the lower swoop of her waist as his hips rose to meet hers and their love-making was just about to hit a crescendo.

He cleared his throat and shifted in his seat. This was all getting a bit too vivid. And why the hell was he being so coy? He stood up against armed *pandilleros* on a regular basis, for heaven's sake. And demanded things. Demanded safety. Protection.

He snorted as he remembered pushing the envelope just that little bit further this morning. A business class ticket for Dr. MacLeay on his journey home. He'd done that for Isla. Demanded it when he had seen the horror in her eyes as she'd tended to the cuts and scrapes her father had received during his "chat" with Axl Cruz. Suffice it to say the man wasn't much of a wordsmith.

Diego looked to the sky, praying for a way to explain to his in-name-only wife that she had, to all intents and purposes, called him her "big boy."

You want to protect her.

He'd known what he was doing when he had

casually talked her through the surgery she'd helped him perform.

Protecting her.

He'd known what he was doing when he'd told her to marry him.

Again. Protecting her.

He'd known *exactly* what he was doing when he'd kissed her at the end of that do-or-die wedding ceremony.

Giving in to an urge that had been building in him from the moment he'd clapped eyes on her.

So why the hell was he protecting her now? When they both knew their marriage was nothing more than a front to save her father?

He didn't want the answer. If he acknowledged the simple fact that his body was waking up from some sort of primordial freeze, he risked opening up his heart to this woman. And that was most definitely *not* on the agenda.

Two separate lives. One pretend marriage. And then they could both go their own ways and leave this insane incident where it belonged. In the past.

"C'mon. What does it mean?" Isla had half turned to him in her seat and prompted, *"Ay, papi!"*

He dove straight into the deep end. "It's something people sometimes say to each other when they are being…*intimate*. Intensely intimate."

Isla's fingers flew to her lips. Lips he had enjoyed tasting more than he cared to admit.

His eyes involuntarily ran the length of her. He would put money on the fact that she didn't have much confidence in herself. The wrinkled skirt and stained T-shirt she'd been wearing when he met her didn't speak of a woman who maximized her appearance over what was inside her head.

Then again...seeing her slender figure in his scrubs... *Muy caliente!*

To him she was utterly beautiful. Her left-of-center looks lit him up right where they shouldn't. From his head to his toes and everywhere in between. He was going to have to squash each and every one of those feelings until Isla was exactly where her father was. Safe and sound on a plane on her way to a country where Noche Blanca would never go. They didn't "do" cold. Doug MacLeay had that on his side. And neither did they risk run-ins with Interpol, whose pockets couldn't be lined.

Diego's eyes flicked to Isla just in time to see fatigue overwhelm her in a series of little head-snaps.

"Right. Time for me to take you home and get you in bed."

She stared at him in horror.

Nice job, Romeo.

CHAPTER FIVE

DIEGO PULLED OFF the scenic coastal road after another ten minutes or so of driving. A thoughtful silence cushioning the air between them.

Or, more to the point, a horrified one.

How had Isla managed to so wildly misinterpret that phrase she'd heard again and again on television? It was more proof, if she'd needed any, of how right she had been to leave Loch Craggen to regroup.

Not that ending up married to a too-handsome stranger with her father winging his way back to Scotland had been anywhere close to the road to recovery she'd envisioned for her battered heart.

Isla forced herself to pay attention to where they were going. Get her physical bearings seeing as her emotional ones were going to remain elusive.

The road they were now on wasn't paved, but it was lined with an avenue of alternating palms and flowering trees that suggested whatever was at the end of the drive had been crafted with care. With longevity in mind.

They turned a corner and she gasped as a beautiful traditional *hacienda* appeared, nestled amidst a sea of flowering buddleia. The building itself was a combination of smoky topaz-colored *adobe*, handmade bricks and some sort of wooden beams that had weathered to a rich burnt umber. The strong earth tones were accented by sunshine and a dazzling array of flower blossoms.

There was a large central archway which was framed by an unearthly-looking bougainvillea. The purest, most deep purple she had ever seen. It reminded her of the type of rich jewel colors a prince might wear. Or a king. It was both beautiful and powerful.

She wrapped her arms round herself and shivered. *Just what had she got herself into?*

Diego parked just outside the archway with a practiced flourish and flashed her a swoon-worthy smile. She silently offered her gratitude that she was sitting down.

"Are we visiting someone?"

He shook his head, a soft smile playing on his lips. "No, *amorcita*."

He stepped out of the car, walked round to her side and held a hand out to her as he opened her door. The way a suitor would. The way her fiancé never had.

"This is your home."

You could have knocked her over with a feather.

"What? Here?"

He turned round to face the *hacienda* alongside her, his hand still encasing hers. "Do you not like it?"

She liked everything about it. It was the kind of place she would have hoped to find if she'd done an internet search for an idyllic Caribbean home.

Talk about a man who played his cards close to his chest…

Suspicion swept away her pleasure. "This isn't something you got through your work with Noche Blanca, is it?"

He huffed out a laugh. "No! No money exchanges hands. *Ever.* But I can't say it's through anything deeply reputable. My family deal in the sugar and coffee trades."

He glared at the house, then turned away. She guessed that meant the subject was closed for discussion. Was he one of "the few who got rich" on the backs of other people's labor?

Something told her that was true. Something else told her it didn't sit well with him.

Diego went to the back of the Jeep and shouldered her bag, which sagged in the middle— bereft, as it was, of clothes.

"You travel light."

She bristled. "I wasn't strictly preparing for a month of captivity." She threw him a haughty look. "If I'd known I would've packed my ball gowns and tiara."

Diego arched an eyebrow. "I'm sure we can rustle up something slightly more appropriate for the wife of one of the island's most prominent doctors than ball gowns or scrubs."

She gave him an apologetic smile when she realized she'd been glaring at him. It wasn't his fault she had packed with her heart rather than her brain. Somewhere way in the back of her wardrobe hung a nice summer dress or two. She screwed her lips up tight. Not that she was dressing up for him or anything.

"Well…" Diego gave her tote a pat. "Your ability to take a trip so spontaneously doubles my respect for your…*resilience* under adversity."

He gave her a small courtly bow, then ushered her toward the covered archway, its edges lined with a few dozen terracotta planters overflowing with ferns and broad-leafed palms.

As she walked under the arch and toward what looked to be a sunlit central courtyard her stomach tightened. Could this experience be something that might actually be *good* for her? A chance to reinvent the woman Kyle had found so boring? So dull? The exact same woman she

knew had it in her to be strong, resilient, coura-
geous. Weren't those traits to admire?

She let her steps fall just a bit behind Diego's
as he led her toward a broad wooden stairwell
that spiraled up to a walkway that ran around the
sunlit courtyard in the center of the house.

"It's absolutely huge. I thought you said you
didn't have any family?"

"I didn't mention it one way or another." He
stopped, his long legs looking even longer as he
leant against the thick wooden banister and gazed
around him. "It's complicated. Would you like to
rest first? Or shall we meet for a coffee on the veranda after you've had a chance to freshen up?"

She looked down at her hands as if they
would give her the answer she was looking for.
She didn't think she was sleepy anymore. Not
with the adrenaline zipping through her body as
countless new questions whirled round her mind.

She felt Diego's gaze upon her before she lifted
her eyes to meet it. He was heavy-lidded. Not
tired. Or judgmental. His long inky lashes barely
contained the heat in his gaze.

A flame burst alight in her very core as his
eyes slowly began to scan the length of her. She
didn't know whether it was fury at being treated
like an ill-gotten gain or... Was it pride? Pride
that a man would look at her with such barely dis-

guised admiration? Though he was a good meter or two away, his gaze felt...*tactile*. Intimate.

She looked down, shocked to realize just how scruffy she looked. Her scrubs were not only stained with the dark red earth that made up the bulk of the unpaved roads, they were stained with Cruzito's blood. She'd completely forgotten that the clothes she'd been wearing would probably be better off being incinerated rather than washed.

Kyle would have insisted she change hours earlier—

She stopped the thought in its tracks. *He's not Kyle. Diego Vasquez is in a league of his own.*

She openly met his gaze, hoping he could see the depths of gratitude she felt that he had saved her father. Saved her. And somehow, in the process of doing it all, hadn't made her feel beholden. Quite the opposite, in fact. He was making her feel as if they were in this together.

She almost laughed.

Imagine! Little Miss Goody Two-Shoes being in cahoots with an off-the-radar doctor for El Valderon's criminal element.

Diego clearly sensed her ricocheting thoughts. He quirked an eyebrow as he waited, the corners of that sensual mouth of his twitching toward a full blown smile.

"Perhaps you'd prefer to take a shower?"

He was teasing her now. She could hear it in

his voice. Playful. Suggestive. All her fault for saying that stupid phrase. *Ay, papi!* She'd have to banish it from her lexicon.

"A shower would be lovely," she said. Much more primly than she'd intended, but there were lines that were not to be crossed.

And one did *not* think saucy thoughts about the man who was effectively her captor when living in his home. That was the rule. And she was sticking to it.

Diego had half a mind to scoop Isla up, carry her the handful of remaining stairs up to his own suite and show her just how satisfying a shower could be.

But he was in his family home and his mother— back when she had cared about such things— had taught him to be respectful of women. That, and he already knew that one hot, soapy shower would only be the start of things. Which was why it was better not to start anything at all.

Visiting medical staff. Tourists looking for a holiday fling. Anyone with a guaranteed departure date. That was what he was interested in.

Isla has a guaranteed departure date.

"Allow me to show you to your room."

She nodded, caught his eye just before he turned away, and in that instant he saw a flash of fear.

A feeling of defensiveness tugged at his chest. He wouldn't hurt her. *Ever.* This was his sanctuary. He loved it here. Valued it. The handful of flings he'd had most certainly hadn't been conducted here, in the family home. This was not a place where he brought people—and yet here he was, guiding in his bride. A woman he'd known half as long as he'd been married to her. Less than a sum total of twenty-four hours. Didn't that speak to the fact that he should never even *think* of laying a hand on her?

She's not here by choice.

"Oh! Señor Diego." The family's long-term housekeeper, Carmela, bustled out of the room he was about to show Isla to. "The room is fixed as you requested. Who was it you were—?"

She stopped abruptly as her eyes lit on Isla. In the blink of an eye her dark gaze took in Isla's scrubs. The blood stains. The shadows under her eyes. The tension in her shoulders. The ring on her finger.

A stranger wouldn't have noticed, but Carmela had known him since he was a boy, and he watched as she registered the peculiarity of the situation and chalked it up to Noche Blanca.

Ever resilient, and prepared to wage resistance against the men who had brought violence to her homeland, Carmela popped on a warm smile and turned her attention fully toward Diego. "What can I do to help?"

Diego could have hugged her. Carmela's loyalty to his family ran in her veins. He knew he could count on her to roll with the… Well, not with the punches, exactly. No one had died. On either side. He had a reluctant bride, and he wasn't exactly dancing with joy either, but big picture? It was a good day.

Bigger picture? He'd figure out a way to deal with Axl. He usually did.

Immediate picture? He needed to look after his wife.

Isla was visibly wilting. Exhaustion was beginning to set in to her slight frame as the clarity of her aqua eyes became shadowed with fatigue. But seeing she wasn't completely alone with him in the house seemed to have given her a sense of comfort.

In Spanish he asked the housekeeper, "Would you mind showing Señora Vasquez her room?"

Carmela didn't arch her eyebrows or suck in a sharp breath. Nor did she comment on the fact that this had been his mother's room. Or that he had addressed the stranger standing on the external balcony as his wife. Instead she did what she always did—treated him like the son she'd never had.

She glared at him as Isla approached the doorway to the suite. *"Que?"* She switched to English. "You're just going to let the poor girl *walk* across the threshold?"

Isla's eyes popped wide open even as Diego narrowed his, only just managing to stem a laugh.

If he was going to come home married and expect Carmela to play along then she was going to call a few shots.

"Of course not." He held out a hand to Isla. *"Mi amor?"*

"What the—?"

"Do you remember when I told you we take marriage seriously here?"

Before she could ask another question Diego swept her into his arms and carried her across the threshold into a room he'd not stepped foot in for over five years.

She wasn't pushing him away. Or struggling to jump out of his arms. So he strode into the room and headed toward the—

Everything had changed.

He'd expected a… Well, a mausoleum wouldn't be the exact word he would've chosen… But Carmela had clearly taken matters into her own hands long before he'd sent her a text message to "freshen up the second master suite".

"I think you're going a bit overboard on the newlywed thing," Isla whisper-growled.

He looked down at her and smiled. "What? You don't like being carried around?"

Her cheeks pinked up. "Not so much."

A devil lit on his shoulder. "Enough to protest...or not so much that you'd refuse me carrying you to your bed?"

She pursed her lips at him. "I think I can manage on my own, thank you very much."

He feigned a short gasp of woe. "Carmela will be very disappointed in me."

"Yes, well..."

She began to wriggle enough for him to concede that it was probably time to put her down.

"I think you probably could've introduced us a bit more...truthfully. That would've been a good way to start. I have a name. A job. A purpose in life other than being your...your...*arm candy.*"

"Carmela understands the situation."

"What?" she whipped round to look at the door, which had discreetly been shut by Carmela. "Have you *told* her? How many people know, exactly?"

"You, me, your father and Carmela."

"And the whole of Noche Blanca?" She stared at him. "Right? That's what this whole charade was for, wasn't it? For Noche Blanca? Making sure my father was safe."

"Sí, amorcita."

She gave her head a sharp shake. "Please don't call me that."

"It's a term of endearment. Like you might use *sweetie* or *honey*."

"Yes. Well… I don't really use those terms. And I think under the circumstances they are wildly inappropriate."

Her discomfort crackled toward him as if he'd cornered her and she'd morphed into a feral cat.

No. The opposite of feral. He knew because he was the same way when cornered. It was loss of control. She didn't like it.

Well, nor did he. It was why he'd snatched back control of a spiraling situation last night. But his knight in shining armor act had taken any sense of control away from her.

They were each trying to find a way to navigate the best path out of this mess, and he owed it to her to let her know that they were on an equal footing. That they were both on foreign territory. The only way they'd get out of this was if they worked as one unit. He huffed out a laugh. Oh, the irony. If they worked as husband and wife.

He took a step back. Gave her the space she so obviously wanted.

"What do you say we take some time to have a rest and then we'll talk everything through? You can ask me anything. Whatever you like."

"What if I'd like to call my government back home and tell them I'm being held under duress?"

A shot of something hot and fiery seared through his chest. "Is that what you think this is? Some sort of *fun* I've been having with you?"

She backed up and bumped into the bed. He'd frightened her. *Dios!* He clawed a hand through his hair, then held up his hands.

"Apologies. There's no excuse for lashing out like that." He dug his fingers into the back of his neck, only to feel knots on top of the knots he'd felt the night before. "Look. We are both exhausted. Why don't we—?"

"I don't want to sleep," she interrupted. "I want to find out what on earth this is all about."

"Good. Fine." He rubbed his hands together. "Compromise?"

She gave him a wary look.

"I need a shower. You probably do, too."

"What? Are you saying I'm *smelly* now?"

Steam was virtually pouring out of her ears. Isla looked absolutely indignant.

His heart… What was his heart doing?

It was aching for her. For this insane situation. For the fear she must be feeling for her father. For… Yes, he might as well say it. For feeling imprisoned.

He had two choices here. Sit down and talk things through right now—and most likely stick his foot straight in it—or walk away, regroup, and talk it through later like a sane person.

"You smell like a spring morning." She didn't have to know he actually believed it.

She snorted. "I'd have to shower for a week to smell anything close to spring."

An image flashed into his mind of silky warm water pouring through Isla's red hair, across her pale skin, over the shifts and curves of her body. Hot blood shot due south of his hips.

Those thoughts were not helping.

"Very well, then. Do as you please." He knew he sounded as if he was dismissing her, but he needed a shower of his own. An icy cold one. "If we meet in the courtyard in an hour, say? Carmela will bring some coffee and we'll have a proper talk. Would that be all right?"

"Perfectly." She gave him a crisp nod.

He turned and left so she wouldn't see his grimace. The foreseeable future was going to be hell.

Not just because of Noche Blanca. They were a nasty irritant but they could be dealt with. The hell would be in reminding himself that he hadn't married this woman for a single reason other than to do his version of taking control. He was showing Axl Cruz he'd met his match. That life would be different now on El Valderon. That the land he'd secretly donated to the turtle sanctuary via a shell corporation was meant to be that. A sanctuary and nothing else.

As he closed the thick cedar door behind him he felt, for the first time in a very long time, that he'd finally met someone who just might truly understand him.

And it scared the hell out of him.

As she watched Diego disappear behind the intricately carved wooden door Isla's fatigue was overridden by her first lucid thought since the entire drama had begun.

There's so much more to him than meets the eye.

She wanted to find out what motivated him. What insane turn of events had pushed him to take these equally mad measures. Marry a stranger to save the life of another one? Her father didn't know Diego. Or at least he didn't seem to.

Seeing Diego interact with the white-haired, clear-eyed housekeeper had opened up yet another side to him she hadn't expected. He was gentle. He liked to make people happy. Carmela was obviously the housekeeper, and yet he treated her like a beloved grandmother, indulging her with that ridiculously old-fashioned carrying the bride over the threshold palaver.

How many more sides to him were there?

She'd seen Diego the hero. The surgeon. The negotiator. The groom.

A lava-hot whorl of heat swirled up from her core and lazily floated around as her fingers traced her lips again. She gave her hands a brisk rub. The kind that was meant to clear those types of thoughts from her head. He was her husband in name only. A means to an end.

And yet…

And yet nothing.

He was a man who picked up his bride and carried her into a *separate* bedroom then walked away. Because he was also a man of his word. He said he wouldn't hurt her. And she believed him.

Standing here on her own was just the reminder she needed that none of this was real. It was a fiction created to get her father safely off the island.

You didn't exactly invite him to stay and test the firmness of the mattress!

She scanned the huge old wooden bed, the richly colored fabrics, the abundance of pillows and a headboard she could imagine clinging to while—

No. She couldn't picture anything of the sort.

A shiver juddered down her spine. She wasn't cold. Quite the opposite. So this was what it felt like to have someone under her skin.

Her spine straightened as yet another niggle from her past leapt to the fore.

Her ex had *never* given her this feeling. In a good or a bad way.

In fact, this was the first time in the past few days she had thought of him without an accompanying sense of…hurt? Betrayal?

She checked her cheeks.

No tears.

She put her hand on her heart.

No pain.

She tried to picture Kyle and…nothing.

So why had she spent a week sobbing into her pillow?

The truth shot through her like adrenaline.

She didn't love him.

She wasn't mourning a broken heart. She was mourning the fact that her sensible plan to get married, have a couple of children and lure her father back home to Loch Craggen had failed.

Until now.

Until Diego.

But her father was there and she was here.

How about that for irony?

The silly part of her—the one she rarely tapped into—stood up and spread her arms wide.

If her life was a musical, she suspected this would be the part where she started singing a hugely inspiring song about seeing the world through fresh eyes.

It would be quiet at first. *A capella*. She'd describe the mind-blowing epiphany of discovering that Kyle *hadn't* driven her from her home. That there'd been no need for her to leave. That she could still hold her head high. That *he* was the liar and the cheat in this scenario.

But he *had* destroyed her ultimate goal. To lure her father back with the promise of a something…*someone*…he might love enough to come home for. *She* obviously wasn't enough. Never had been. But grandchildren? Who could resist grandchildren?

It was all so clear now. Sobbing and bashing her pillow into submission hadn't been heartbreak over Kyle. It had been frustration that her father had, once again, prioritized his work over her. Even when she'd come to him virtually carrying her heart in both hands, saying, *Look. It's broken. Fix it.*

She'd truly believed he would fix it by throwing in the towel and agreeing to accompany her back to Loch Craggen.

Pffft. Showed her.

Turtles: One.

Isla: Nil.

Or was it one point each to Noche Blanca and the turtles? Either way it still left her at nil.

The more she thought about it, the more she realized this song of hers was going to be *really* long. More like an epic Nordic saga, involving travels to strange worlds, battles with evil clans, and confrontations of the totally mind-boggling variety with a drop-dead gorgeous surgeon who appeared like a Latin Poseidon in the midst of a storm.

Or a very close variation on that theme.

Diego *was* disarmingly attractive. Not that she'd spent all that much time noticing when her survival had been on the line, but now that it was down to just him, her and Carmela…

Oof. This was going to be a long month.

She gave the room another scan. It was completely plausible that a movie star might live here. Or a billionaire. Or both. It was the total opposite of her plain Jane bedroom back home. White walls. White sheets. White duvet cover.

The floor wasn't white. There was that… But this room was everything hers wasn't. Both a riot of color and the most soothing place she'd ever been.

It was huge. The size of her entire wee house back home.

The walls were a rich, buttery yellow. Naturally aged beams that looked as though they had borne witness to more than a century of Vasquez family history spanned the length of the room.

There were thick teak chairs cushioned up to the hilt with jewel-colored pillows, set beside a set of French windows that led out to a balcony overlooking a ridiculously perfect sea view. Fresh flowers nestled in thick ceramic jugs and scented the air.

It was the type of place she'd never even thought to imagine herself visiting, let alone calling home.

This isn't your home. This is temporary.

She pressed her eyes tight shut as she sank onto the edge of the huge bed. A large, dark wooden-framed number that could have accommodated an entire family. At the end of it was a huge wooden chest with thick cast-iron clasps. The type of chest a woman from another era might have put her trousseau in. Or her wedding dress…stored away to share with her daughter one day…

An image popped into her mind of Diego, a swarm of children and…oh, goodness…*her*. Right there. On the bed. With all of them. Laughing. Smiling. Tickling. Hugging.

She shoved the image to one side and brought up the much more real memory of her father waving to her as he went through Security and disappeared into the crowd.

"You can do this," he'd whispered to her during their final hug. "You can save the turtles."

She wasn't one to resent an animal on the verge of extinction, but…*really?* It had been a much greater emotional blow than she'd imagined. Perhaps that was why she was being so snappy with Diego who, in fairness, deserved nothing but kindness for all he'd done.

She'd picked up her heart, stuffed it back into her chest and only stiffened a little bit when Diego had tried to wrap her in his arms and comfort her. In all honesty, she was frightened. Frightened to let those pent-up demons loose. Once she began to cry about the parents who'd never really valued her she wasn't sure she'd ever stop.

A soft knock sounded on the door. "*Señora?* It's me… Carmela."

She reluctantly pushed herself away from the bed and opened the door.

Carmela came in with Isla's bag over one shoulder and a big box that looked as if it was from an old-fashioned department store over the other.

"Señor Vasquez has asked me to bring you your things."

Isla rushed over to help unload Carmela. She took the bag, and Carmela crossed to the wooden chest and placed the box on top.

"Erm…this isn't mine."

She winced apologetically. This was so weird. Worse than being caught at a boyfriend's house by his parents wearing nothing but her bra and panties. Not that it had ever happened to her, because she was incredibly cautious in that department, but she was pretty sure this was what it would have felt like.

Carmela, however, seemed completely unfazed. As if mystery brides were always showing up unannounced and in need of protection.

The thought made her blood boil. She could have got herself out this mess her own way, given half a chance!

No, you couldn't. You needed him.

"These are some things Señor Vasquez thought you might need." Carmela looked at Isla with more than casual interest. "Can I get you anything?"

Nineteen different responses crowded in her throat. Her father, for one. Her old life. Her patient roster. Her cozy little home by a very different sea, where a half-eaten packet of biscuits lay in her favorite tin alongside the hot chocolate. She could definitely do without Kyle. Or any boyfriends/fiancés/love interests for the foreseeable future. But…

She swallowed them all down and felt a pang of discomfort in her gut as they landed.

Did she *really* want those things? Or was this crazy scenario something she'd needed for a bit longer than she cared to admit? A chance to challenge herself to become the woman she'd always wanted to be? Fierce. Independent. Worthy of being loved.

She shook her head. "No, thank you. Everything's perfect."

"He's a good man, you know," Carmela said.

There was no need to ask who she was speaking about. A prickle of tears began to tease at the back of Isla's nose. She nodded her head. She knew that. She owed Diego a debt she could never repay. The debt of her life.

How soon would she owe him the debt of her freedom?

Carmela gave her arm a gentle squeeze. One that said, *I'm here for you if you need me.*

"Diego will see you in the courtyard in an hour's time. Perhaps some rest will help."

Like the ever-obedient child she'd crafted herself into, Isla sat down on the bed as Carmela left the room. Exhaustion hit her like a speeding train the moment the kind woman gently closed the door behind her. The bedding was unbelievably soft to the touch. If she lay down for just one sleepy second…

Diego stayed for a moment. He knew he shouldn't. That watching someone sleep might be seen as intrusive, but… *Dios mio*, the woman's beauty clawed at heart.

And she wasn't just anyone. She was his *wife*. *In name only, idiota!*

A shot of unease curdled his relief at finally being home.

Axl Cruz was hardly high on the scale of globally feared gangsters. He'd barely register as a tiny dot on Interpol's radar. But here on El Valderon... Diego's hand automatically moved to his chest. The emotional scars upon his heart were traces of just how close to the bone Axl Cruz and his so-called "mischief-making" could cut. The man had to be stopped.

He pulled a light blue throw from the end of the bed, put it and over Isla's shoulders. She didn't deserve any of this. Nor did her father, for that matter. But Isla was a true innocent. He reached out, giving in to the urge to sweep an errant curl away from her face. She shifted and put her fingers alongside his. Squeezed them as if she knew he was there to help, gave a soft sigh, then curled her hands together over her heart.

He knew then and there that he would do everything in his power to protect her. To help her. And then he would let her go.

CHAPTER SIX

ISLA BLINKED HER eyes open and wondered how the room had gone from being filled with the warm glow of filtered sunlight to cozy and gently lit by a standing lamp in the corner. She examined the blue blanket that was wrapped around her and tried to remember covering herself with it. Unsuccessfully.

She bolted upright, suddenly remembering where she was and from whom she was meant to be nailing down some actual facts.

She squinted toward the French windows as her brain registered that the sun was slipping below the horizon. She must have been asleep for hours, and she was meant to be insisting that Diego take her to an embassy. If there even *were* any. This country was so isolated. Its government so new.

"The walls have ears, amorcita."

It was what he'd said when she'd starting flinging insults about Axl Cruz, after they'd finished operating on his son. Not her finest moment, but…

She rose and immediately realized that a shower was going to be essential before she went anywhere or did anything. She went to her bag and pulled out her lone skirt and T-shirt.

Filthy.

She hadn't yet figured out where the laundry facilities were at the turtle sanctuary...*ugh*. At least she had clean underwear. She'd been thorough in that department.

She glanced out the window at the setting sun. Her father should be landing any time now.

Home.

How cruel that her father should finally be there while she was stuck here in this— Well... She'd landed on her feet in terms of enforced captivity.

Her eyes slid across to the large box. She lifted the lid and gasped as she saw a pile of clothes.

There were lovely light cotton and linen tops. Some with pretty flower patterns. Some richly colored in shades of blue and green. Pedalpushers and cropped trousers in neutral colors. A couple of swingy shift dresses she would never in her wildest dreams have had the courage to buy herself.

She held one up to her shoulders and stepped in front of the long mirror in the bathroom.

She actually sighed at how pretty it looked. How pretty *she* looked. And she just about *never* thought of herself as pretty. She'd wear it tonight. Only because she wouldn't ever be wearing it again, seeing as she would be putting her foot down and insisting they sort out this insane situation and get her back home with her father, where she belonged.

One luxuriously satisfying shower later and she gave herself a final glimpse in the mirror.

She was surprised to see how vital she looked. How alive. The color green Diego had chosen—or whoever he'd asked to choose for him had chosen—suited her fair skin and dark auburn hair to perfection. The wrap-around dress was form-fitting, but not so much that she felt she needed to suck in her tummy or worry about any strange bulges that might have appeared on her thighs after a bit of over-indulgent chocolate consumption the night she'd found out that she had been cuckolded.

She'd never felt more humiliated in her life. Or more furious.

Reluctantly, she conceded that maybe her ex had had a point. She'd been so set on her vision of how the future had to be that she had forgotten how to be spontaneous. Her drive and ambition to become an emergency medicine specialist had been channeled into her girlhood dream of playing Happy Families in Loch Craggen.

But what if her family's version of Happy Families was actually what it *was*? Everyone free to pursue their dreams?

She shook her head. Too much to think about. Tonight she had to quiz Diego.

She took a quick glance in the mirror again and gave her hair a stern warning not to go feral in the warm sea air. She needed to be at her persuasive best tonight, and if that involved employing her disturbingly under-utilized feminine wiles, then…

She caught the flash of her ring in the mirror. The ring that had come just before the exchange of vows that had come just before the most passionate kiss she'd ever had in her life.

Her tummy flipped and little bits of her tingled that she hadn't realize could tingle.

Crikey.

She was going to have to pretend Diego looked like a frog when she spoke to him.

Frogs turn into princes. And princes turn into Beasts.

Reminding herself that she was an immensely sensible woman with a very clear agenda—departure—she walked to the outdoor patio, to find Diego looking towards the sea into the embers of daylight.

"Ah! Isla. Are you feeling well rested? A bit more relaxed?"

She was feeling *something*, all right, but she wasn't sure it was relaxed.

The golden remains of the sun highlighted his warm, caramel-colored skin and the shiny black of his hair—still a bit wild and disheveled, even though his change of clothes and freshly shaved face indicated that he'd showered. She caught her fingers in their first full-on act of betrayal. They were itching to touch his hair. Touch *him*.

Which was why turning around and leaving when she felt him all but devouring her with his eyes was the wisest course of action.

She pulled herself up short.

"Would Señora Vasquez like a glass of wine?"

Isla stared at Carmela, wondering how on earth she'd appeared on the seaside patio without so much as a whisper of a noise.

"Isla, please. *Por favor*. Please call me Isla." She tried to add a message with her eyes… *Could you also rescue me from this sexy man? My husband?*

"*Si, señora*. Would you like a glass of wine? Or some *sangria*?"

Her throat was scratchy and dry. "*Sangria* would be lovely," she croaked.

She glanced back at Diego and saw he was still looking at her through eyes cast down at half-mast. He wasn't judging—he was assessing. And when his lifted his gaze to meet hers she saw an insatiable hunger in them.

Why had she worn the dress? She should have worn the pedal-pushers and the one long-sleeved top she'd found in the treasure trove of new clothes.

He blinked, and when he opened his eyes again they were cool. Completely absent was the heat she was certain she'd seen burning bright in them not milliseconds ago. Ice-cold. As if she were little more than someone he was obliged to greet when they passed one another in the street.

"I trust you slept well?"

It was a simple enough question. Yet she found she was standing there like a mute idiot.

How stark a reminder did she need that Diego was someone who played by a different set of rules? Rules that knew justice wasn't always found at the bottom of a judge's gavel.

She dropped her gaze to his mouth. A mouth that could be cruel at the flip of a coin. And ridiculously sensual if it was crashing down on a woman's mouth and claiming her as his own. For example...

Well, she was simply going to have to ignore his mouth. And his hair. And every other damn attractive thing about him.

"Are you all right, Isla?"

Diego had the cheek to switch moods again.

Act as if he cared. Well, he could just bloody carry on trying. She was immune to him and his chameleon nature.

She crossed her arms and nodded. Sure. She was A-Okay. Wasn't *every* woman who had just gone through one of the most traumatic events of her life and then found herself married and captive in an absolutely perfect *hacienda* by the sea?

He crossed to her and led her to a nearby oak bench, piled abundantly with peacock-colored pillows and cushions.

"Here. Take a seat. Carmela will be back with your drink soon. Would you like some water?"

He lifted a jug weighted with water, the cool beads of perspiration on the outside of the dark blue glass indicating it was icy cold. She had half a mind to grab it and pour it on top of herself. Or him. But all she could do was nod, silently thanking the heavens that he didn't know what was going on in her brain.

One glass of water later she had knocked some proper Scottish common sense back into herself.

"So..." She sat primly on the edge of the bench, which was all but begging her to lean back into its pile of cushions with a sigh and a smile. "I suppose we have a fair amount of territory to cover..."

Diego lifted one of his eyebrows, amusement

dancing through his eyes. "That's one way to put it."

He glanced into the house, then took a seat on a deep armchair catty-corner to her. His knees nearly touched hers. She shifted in the opposite direction. If they were going to do this, he was going to have to respect her personal space!

"Right." She gave her lap a little pat with her hands. "I suppose you could start by telling me who you really are."

"Are we talking on an existential level or just bare bones facts?"

Diego enjoyed watching Isla's hackles fly up and then swiftly, as she clocked his dry tone, seeing her frown straighten into a *ha-ha, very funny* smirk. A swell of pride that he'd eased the tension in those two little furrows between her eyebrows needled his resolve to keep this entire conversation as neutral as possible.

"Facts will do perfectly well, thank you very much." She gave a curt nod.

She was adorable when she was being prim. But he wouldn't belittle her by more teasing. Heaven knew, the woman had been through more than enough over the past twenty-four hours. But by God he was tempted. Her smile was far more rewarding than her frown.

"*Ahora.* Shall I start at the beginning? Or are

you happy if I give you a quick overview and then you can ask questions from there?"

"Quick overview," she said, without a moment's hesitation.

"Don't you want any time to think about that?"

She shot him a look.

There went his vow not to tease her anymore. He quite liked it—seeing the flash of frustration, the quick dawning of recognition, the sharp wit whirling away behind those blue eyes of hers, the smile that brought out a tiny dimple in her left cheek.

"Right—"

He stopped as Carmela slid cool drinks onto the tiled table between them and left the semi-enclosed patio area as silently as she'd appeared. He swore the woman must have been a trained ninja in a past life. And a Michelin-starred chef. He made a quick mental note to ask her to cook one or two of his favorites for Isla. He'd love to see her reaction to them.

He pulled his eyes away from Isla's lips as they parted to draw in a cool draught of the *sangria* and forced himself to start speaking again. This wasn't business. But it most distinctly wasn't—couldn't be—pleasure. Not only would he feel as if he was taking advantage of Isla, he'd be breaking a seven-year vow to avenge his brother's death with the one thing Axl Cruz would loathe: peace.

"Fifteen years ago the government of El Valderon changed. But the new government has struggled to hold on to power."

"What is the biggest problem?"

"It needs a strong leader who can guide the country away from its colonial past. The rich are still rich and the poor are still for the most part very poor."

He watched as Isla's eyes scanned the beautifully appointed courtyard. This place oozed old money. After his parents' marriage had fallen to pieces, in the wake of Nico's death, he'd quietly taken the reins and turned most of his family's enterprises into more community friendly affairs. Fairtrade. Co-ops.

But there were a lot of hurdles yet to cross before they were truly egalitarian. And not everyone was happy with his plan to employ known Noche Blanca members.

Memories ran long and deep on El Valderon. It would take generations before the Vasquez name wasn't accompanied by a sneer. Over the past few hundred years they had done much more harm than good.

Isla was looking at him. Silently. Expectantly.

"I don't think I need to say which side of the coin my family were on."

"The gold-plated one?" Isla asked with a glint in her eye.

He nodded.

"Well, lucky me." She didn't sound as though she felt lucky. "Landing the island's most eligible bachelor."

He barked out a laugh. It was obvious she was trying to be narky. Funnily enough, it felt refreshing to have someone not treating him like royalty.

"Suffice it to say that when we go out tomorrow you will be on the receiving end of—"

"Wait a minute," Isla cut in sharply. "What do you mean, when we go out tomorrow? I thought I'd be holed up like Rapunzel or Briar Rose for the next thirty days."

All signs of humor dropped from his face as he leant forward, elbows on knees, and looked her straight in the eye. "I know what happened last night might seem a million miles away—"

"On the contrary," she bridled. "It's all still feeling very real! This time last night I was destined for spinsterhood and a life of giving unwelcome lectures on the merits of a low-fat diet for the rest of my life, all the while wondering if my father was dead or alive."

There was a lot of information there. Spinsterhood? Fear for her father? Had she suspected he was somewhere dangerous? What had prompted her to come if she knew it was dangerous?

You would've faced a firing squad if it would have saved Nico.

He wasn't going to touch on her love-life. Too personal. That, and he didn't really like the idea of Isla with another man. He went for as neutral a comment as he could.

"He's a bit of an eco-warrior, your father."

Her eyebrows shot up as high as they would go. "That's putting it mildly. He's like a one-man army. If my mother hadn't—" She clapped her hand over her mouth, shook her head, then reached for her glass and took another long drink.

Had her eyes filled up? Whatever had happened with her mother, she didn't want to talk about it. Fair enough. Mothers was a complicated topic for him too.

His mother managed to appear here at the *hacienda* once a year at best. Usually with the pretense of giving him a surprise birthday party, though the dates never actually coincided. He knew as well as she did that grown men didn't really need their mothers to throw them birthday parties. And she never refused the transfer he always put into whatever international bank account she accidentally-on-purpose mentioned "in passing."

"Are you in touch with her? Your mother?" he asked Isla.

"No."

He clearly wasn't getting any more than that. Fair enough. This was supposed to be about her current predicament, not her past.

"I thought you should come with me when I go to work at the hospital tomorrow. Seeing as news will travel fast that you're my new bride."

"Wait... At the hospital? And how on earth will anyone know we're—?" She stopped herself as her ring caught the light of the stained-glass table lamp and threw a rainbow on her face. "The airport." She answered her own question. "We were together at the sanctuary and the airport. I still don't understand why Axl Cruz didn't oversee that himself... My father's departure."

"It's a power thing. He wants people to know your father was doing his bidding. Word would have spread about Cruzito and Axl would have seen taking no action as a sign of weakness."

"But my father wasn't the one to shoot him," Isla protested.

"No, but one of the security guards he was paying did."

She gold-fished for a minute, then asked, "So why do we need to go to the hospital?"

"One—because I work there. Two—I run a mobile clinic which I think you would find interesting."

"I can't believe the hospital employs you when

they must know you also work for those…those *criminals*."

He felt the familiar wash of darkness cloud his heart. "I treat *patients*. Besides…" He heard his voice turn as crisply efficient as hers had earlier. "I don't work for Axl Cruz. Nor do I draw a salary from the hospital. As you can see, I have ample wealth. I want for nothing. I work for *me*. That's it."

She absorbed his tone, the stony features, the rigid set of his shoulders, and nodded. "Of course. I see."

He could tell that she didn't. That she knew there was something more. And that she was frightened enough by his dark mood-swing not to press.

Just tell her about your brother!

He took a long draught of his drink, then refilled both their glasses. He wasn't used to this. Having someone to talk with. Someone he could genuinely confide in. Carmela knew everything about him, making talking to her a moot point. Besides, she and her family were dependent on him. It automatically created a barrier between them.

Unlike that perfectly natural marriage at gunpoint you shared with Isla…

She'd not shown fear. She'd shown resourcefulness. And right now she was sitting here, waiting for him to give her a damn good explanation as to what had happened last night and why the hell he had plans to parade her around El Valderon.

So he told her the truth.

"Seven years ago my brother died. The hospital refused to send an ambulance when they heard he was the victim of a gunshot wound."

She sat forward in her chair and the space she'd obviously tried to keep between them dissolved. "You mean he was part of Noche Blanca?"

"No. It's more complicated than that." He drained his glass again. "When he was a teenager Nico had meningococcal septicemia."

"He was lucky he didn't die."

"He *did* die," Diego bit out. "That's the point."

Isla's brows cinched together as she waited for him to flesh out the story.

He drew a ragged breath, then continued. "Nico was the family favorite. He was a few years younger than me. The puppy I never had."

"Interesting analogy."

"Are you an only child?"

She nodded.

A wistful smile hit him, and left just as suddenly. "Suffice it to say, little brothers are like happy-go-lucky puppies with big dreams. Nico bewitched us all with his plans for the future. He was going to be an architect. Draw tourists to El Valderon with his whimsical creations. He was hoping he would open art museums and restaurants, showcasing local food and crafts. He was friends with everyone. Especially young men his own age who were…vulnerable. Easily persuaded."

"Easily persuaded by Axl Cruz?"

"One and the same. Long story short: Axl used to live on another island. He was big in the petty crime department there until a bigger man from a bigger island moved in. It's the way it seems to work. Turf-building. So Axl moved here, sensing a weak link as we moved toward democracy. A lot of the jobs that were manual had been mechanized or consolidated when the last government took over. Axl collected the unemployed, made them hangers-on. Then Nico fell ill and my world changed."

"That's when you decided to become a doctor?"

"*Sí. Exacto.* I had originally planned to follow in my father's footsteps. Run the family business. Provide for future generations of the Vasquez family and, of course, the people of El Valderon. I knew things were changing. My father didn't. But when Nico was ill I felt so powerless…"

His eyes caught and cinched with Isla's, but just as quickly he tore them away. He didn't want to feel vulnerable. Not now. Not ever.

In a monotone he continued. It was a painful

story to tell and very few people tore it out of him. And by very few he meant only Isla.

"The meningitis damaged his brain. He was permanently a fourteen-year-old boy from that point on. He got mixed up with Noche Blanca, but not for the reasons most people thought. He was vulnerable. Wanted to be friends with anyone. Thought he could convince everyone to be friends with him. One day he got caught in the crossfire between Axl's oldest son and a shopkeeper. The boys were idiots. Untrained and wielding weapons they had no business having. There was too much chaos, and the hospital didn't want to risk the lives of their staff."

"So that's why you began to help Noche Blanca once you'd finished med school?"

How did she do it? See straight into his soul? As obvious as it was to him, not one single person had ever connected the dots. *Not. One.*

People had thought quite the opposite. That he'd become a lawyer. Go into politics. Anything that could help him wreak revenge. But he didn't want revenge. He wanted change.

"Got it in one."

"And has working with Noche Blanca helped?"

He shook his head. Some days he thought yes. Other days he didn't have a clue.

Isla's lips eased into a conspiratorial smile.

"Keep your friends close and your enemies closer?"

He returned the smile. "Something like that."

"Fair enough."

Unexpectedly, she laughed.

"What?"

"Your situation reminds me of trying to get one of my patients to quit smoking. Dougray Campbell. We have a deal. Each year he'll take his daily count down by one."

"Slow and steady wins the race?"

She nodded. She was trying to tell him she understood. That she knew the changes he passionately sought wouldn't happen overnight.

He raised his glass. She lifted hers to meet his and together they drank. Their first toast as a married couple. To understanding how complicated the world was.

"So..." Isla put her glass down and looked him straight in the eye. "Seeing as you're keeping me even closer, what does that make me? A frenemy?"

"My wife."

Her flush of response pummeled any perspective he might have had on the scenario to smithereens.

"Right." Isla gave her lap a decisive pat. "If we're to go to the hospital for you to show me off,

I'd like to make it very clear I'm not planning on lying around eating bonbons."

"Oh, no." If there was one thing he was certain about, the only way she'd be leaving this house would be under his watchful eye. And he couldn't do that at work. "You can consider yourself on holiday for the next month. Your honeymoon."

"Not without you taking precisely the same honeymoon, I'm not."

She could see from his gritted teeth that he wasn't going to be honeymooning anytime soon.

"I'm not just a show pony. I want to work."

"I see." He adopted a casual air, pulling his ankle atop his knee before leaning back into his chair. "And what is it, exactly, that you plan on doing?"

She ticked points off on her fingers. "I'd like to make sure the sanctuary stays safe. The best way to do that would be for me to be there. All day. Every day."

"No." She wouldn't be safe there. Not on her own.

She ignored him. "Turtles aren't really my thing, though, and, as such, I'd like to turn my father's bungalow into a health clinic."

"Absolutely not."

"Yes. Absolutely *yes*." She glared at him and made a *zip your lip* gesture. "I think this clinic should be about preventative medicine rather than emergency medicine. It should sending a message that I'm here to *prevent* bad things from happening—not cause them."

She would be sending a message, all right. One straight to the heart of a community that ached for peace.

"Don't you think you'd be better off doing this at the hospital?" He wanted her to say yes. *Needed* her to say yes. Not that he should care. He refused to let himself care about her.

Then why did you step in and marry the woman?

"No," she said.

He lifted his hands to the heavens. *Surprise, surprise.*

"As I said, I'd like to keep an eye on the sanctuary and it's the best way for me to do that."

"People will be frightened to go there right now. Perhaps if you start at the mobile clinic I run for the hospital and move over to the sanctuary once you've made your point it would be better…"

He left out the part about how much he wanted her close to him, where he could keep an eye on her. Protect her. He knew Axl would back off the land for a few days, but after that… He simply had no guarantees.

Her smile and casual shrug told him she'd take

his advice under consideration. But ultimately He knew she was through being told what to do.

"I want to make a splash."

"Oh, you'll definitely do that." He downed the rest of his drink in one. "El Valderon won't know what's hit it."

CHAPTER SEVEN

ISLA WOKE WITH a surprising amount of zing in her step.

Taking charge of one's own destiny and wearing yet another new dress that fit like a dream had a way of adding a bit of kick to a girl's attitude.

That, and—although she was a bit shocked to admit it—so was wearing sexy underwear she never ever would have chosen if left to her own devices.

Gone were the plain-Jane matching bra and panties sets she normally bought at the supermarket. The lingerie she wore today was in another league from her regular cotton panties and bra of dubious assistance. It was *lingerie*, not underwear. Sexy silk and lace lingerie, in bold jewel colors.

Was this how Diego imagined her? As a woman whose skin knew only silk and the finest of lace? A part of her was horrified to think he knew exactly what she was wearing under the dress. But another part... Another part felt emboldened that he saw her as a woman, rather than the boring old plod who always did the dishes and made sure her other half's dinner was hot, no matter what time of night he wandered in.

She shot a glare at her invisible ex-fiancé and flicked her hair. *See? Not everyone thinks I'm boring.*

She looked at herself in the long mirror and slid her hands along her sides, over her curves, more aware than she'd ever been of how *feminine* she felt dressed this way. How strong.

By choosing these clothes Diego was telling her he saw strength in her. Beauty.

No wonder she had extra zing.

And she knew where the bulk of that energy was going to go.

In showing Axl Cruz precisely what happened when you pushed around a woman from Loch Craggen.

She gave herself a silly grin in the mirror. As if she'd be doing it all on her own! Having Diego Vasquez as her ally—*her husband*—would make all the difference. Particularly as he'd made it more than clear that his entire aim was to bring peace to the island.

When she went down the outdoor staircase that curved into the internal courtyard her heart-rate sped up a notch when she saw Diego was already having coffee at a tile mosaic table.

He looked up. Heat flared in his eyes when they lit on her.

She swished her way down the stairs as if she were a movie star. Something about him made her want to show off a little. Make him proud to call her his wife—even if it *was* just a fiction.

Or was it just plain old chemistry? They hadn't stayed up half the night comparing medical school stories just because they cracked each other up. Well, they did that too. But she knew she'd stayed up talking to him because there was a huge part of her that was wondering if he wanted to kiss her as much as she wanted to kiss him.

A chaste kiss had brought the evening to a close when she'd no longer been able to hide her yawns.

The sparks that had followed and sent her running for her room had given "chaste" a whole new definition.

"That's a nice dress."

She gave him a twirl at the bottom of the stairs suddenly acutely aware that moves like this—girly, swirly whirls, making her vividly aware of the feel of the fabric on her skin—were incredibly out of character.

"You're fifty shades of boring!"

Not in Diego's eyes.

Meeting him had been like unzipping an ill-fitting suit and discovering there was a whole different woman inside her. A woman she could admire.

Her spirits sank as quickly as they'd risen. If only her father felt the same.

"You're up early."

She glanced at the large grandfather clock behind Diego. It wasn't *that* early. "Have you already been out?"

He rose from his seat and gestured at the chair across from him, waiting until she sat before continuing. "Paz Cruz. He needed his dressings changed. His medication."

Out of instinct Isla asked for his stats and then, as Diego rattled them off, realized she wished she'd been there too. She didn't like the idea that she and her father might have been discussed. Or that Diego might have undergone some sort of interrogation about his shotgun wedding.

Officially, of course, the marriage could be annulled. There had been no sex. Would be no sex.

She hid behind an eggshell-blue coffee mug and looked at the man who had saved her life by becoming her husband. He was honorable. Proud. With a core of courage and strength. Her father had been right. Of all the men in all the world to be in this particular one-in-a-gazillion scenario with Diego was the man she would have picked.

But she wasn't picking. And she wasn't developing feelings for him. She was going to be sensible and count down the days, then go home and never think about this again.

"When are we going to work?"

He gave her a dry smile and nodded at the cafetière, still half full of coffee. "We islanders like to properly fuel up before we tend to our sick." He indicated a hand-woven basket brimming with tiny pastries. "Want one?"

She laughed. "This is exactly the type of food I try and tell my patients to avoid."

He shrugged and placed it in front of her. "Indulge. You're on your honeymoon."

She pursed her lips but felt tendrils of heat creep into her cheeks in defiance of her cavalier *yeah, right* attitude. A reminder of the saucy thoughts that had kept her awake for far too long in her much too empty bed...

When she had finally nodded off she'd dreamt of him. Definitely something new to tick off on the old sexy bucket list.

Not that she'd ever had one.

Maybe she *had* been one or two of shades of boring...

She bit into a pastry, moaning with pleasure at the buttery hit of sugar, fruit and pastry.

"That's more like it," Diego murmured, his deliciously throaty accent sending her nervous system into overdrive. "Eat up, *mi amor*. We've got a big day ahead of us."

Eyes glued to hers, Diego scraped a crumb of pastry off his lower lip with his tongue. How the man infused the most pedestrian of moves with sex was beyond her.

Her eyes pinged open as a thought occurred to her. If, by some insane turn of events, he were to kiss her right now she'd be powerless to resist. More than that. She wouldn't *want* to.

It was just as well Isla had said she wanted to check out a few things in the hospital foyer. The atmosphere between Diego and Maria was... prickly at best.

"And just who *is* that woman, exactly?"

"She's my wife," he repeated, doing his level-best to keep his tone neutral.

How the hell he'd become so defensive about his fake wife in front of his real employer was beyond him, but he knew one thing for sure. He didn't want anyone referring to Isla as "that woman". She had more integrity in her little finger than most people showed in a lifetime, so he'd be damned if he was going to let Maria shoot the idea down before she heard him out.

"Doug MacLeay's daughter. It was all very fast. Unexpected. But I am sure you will join me in welcoming her both to El Valderon and here at the hospital. She's hoping to make quite a difference in the mobile clinic."

The clinic he and Maria fought about endlessly. She saw it as wasted money. He saw it as an invaluable resource.

"I suppose she'll want to be paid?" Maria threw down her proverbial pair of aces.

"No. She's happy to volunteer." He trumped her with a royal flush.

A cruel man would have enjoyed the shot of fury in Maria's eyes as she absorbed the news. Diego took no pleasure in it. He simply wanted to go to work and keep Isla safe in the process.

He was about to embark on what he was certain would be an unwelcome monologue, flaunting Isla's merits, when—as if she knew he might go off-piste—Isla walked across from the entryway, where she'd been looking at some of the health notices.

Diego introduced them.

"It's a pleasure to meet you." Isla looked Maria straight in the eye. "I'm really looking forward to working in the mobile clinic."

Any pretense of charm Maria had been trying to maintain dropped away. "I'm afraid we really don't have the funding to cover your insurance. And, of course, you'll have to sit our medical exam. It's very rigorous. It'll take weeks, if not months to organize. And as you're newlywed I suppose time is at a premium for you?"

"Fair enough." Isla smiled brightly. "Seeing as that's the case here, I'm assuming it won't be a problem for you if I open up a wellness clinic out at the turtle sanctuary?"

Diego almost laughed. Isla wasn't just delivering a blow to Maria, she was giving *him* the proverbial heave-ho as well. Kudos to her for knowing her own mind.

"Wellness clinic?" Maria didn't even try to rein in her disdain.

"I run a similar program back in Scotland. Just a couple of low-cost clinics a week. I find a preventative approach to medicine cuts back on a lot of unnecessary trips to the emergency ward. It's a way to put a fast track on people prone to diabetes, heart disease, chronic respiratory problems—that sort of thing. Catching preventable diseases late proves very expensive for us, as it involves having to get patients back to the mainland via helicopter or boat. I suspect it's the same for you. I've found the clinic to be a most cost-effective investment. Not to mention its use as a means of catching various cancers early, and lung disease, hypercholesterolemia—"

"Fine. You've painted the picture." Maria glanced at Diego, visibly annoyed at Isla's commonsense plan.

If Diego hadn't been so keen to keep Isla within eyesight—or at least earshot—for the foreseeable future he would've applauded her.

"Turtles *and* people. *Aren't* you from an interesting family?" Maria flicked an invisible piece of lint off her shoulder.

"Diego certainly thought so." Isla smiled benignly. "Didn't you, *mi amor*?"

She looked up at him with a look so pure and loving he would have sworn she meant it. *¡Dios mio!* The woman could've been a politician!

Diego put his arm round his wife's shoulders, a smile twitching at his lips as she snuggled up almost conspiratorially beneath it. They'd make a hell of a team if she weren't here under duress. If she actually cared about him. About the island.

Then again, if this was Isla under pressure he couldn't begin to imagine what she'd be like unleashed.

"Maria, it might be worth considering the excellent PR that would come from launching such a forward-looking program in the mobile clinic. Of course I'd be busy seeing patients of my own there, but if you were to be happy using Isla's British medical license as sufficient evidence of her ability to practice medicine you could announce her intention to meet preventative care patients. There's more than enough room. And if there were any problems I would be on hand to help. Smooth over any transitional problems."

"Our diagnosticians are already overwhelmed with their work here at the hospital…"

It was a flimsy excuse and everyone knew it. The term *grasping at straws* sprang to mind.

"A press release would be brilliant!" Isla leant in to Maria, praising her as if the idea had been her own. "You can assure the press that I'm used to working with limited resources. A stethoscope, a blood pressure cuff and a thermometer work wonders. There would be zero draw on the hospital's resources."

Maria scowled, but didn't storm off as she often did when she and Diego discussed preventative care. She would be perfectly happy for Diego to run a similar clinic so long as he stopped helping Noche Blanca. The argument ended the same way every single time: *Not until we treat everyone the same.*

Maria gave Isla a cursory up-and-down eye-flick. She too operated a policy of keeping her friends close and her enemies closer.

"What if you have no patients and Diego is overloaded? Do you plan on sitting around filing your nails?"

Her hostile approach would have made many women run for the hills. He'd seen it before with Maria. Hackles flew up. Claws came out. Whoever she was speaking to would take their services elsewhere. To a different island, even. But not Isla.

Shrugging out from underneath his arm, she took a step toward Maria and solemnly shook her head no. "Absolutely not. It would be a privilege to work with my husband. Ease his burden. And, of course, help the people of El Valderon."

Diego had to stop himself from letting out a low whistle of approval. His wife gave as good as she got—but with kindness and fairness at the fore.

"Even plasters cost money—who will cover *that*?"

The crack in Maria's voice told him she was beginning to flounder.

"I will," he said.

Any profits Vasquez Corp made were plowed right back into the community, and he was pretty sure this counted. He made a mental note to call the head of the board—a woman who doled out fair solutions as rigorously and passionately as she worked picking coffee beans.

"Dropping money on vanity projects? Picking up wives in the course of a weekend?" Maria snapped. "It's all so easy for you, isn't it?"

Diego dropped any pretense of charm. "No, Maria. It isn't. The instant my brother died any sort of ease I had with the world evaporated."

The blood drained from Maria's face, and as she drew in a sharp breath to launch her rebuttal attack Isla stepped between the pair of them, instantly defusing the near-explosive tension with a quick nod and a clap of her hands.

"Right, then," she said. "If it's all right with the pair of you, I'd like to get to work."

"Well done, *mi amor*."

Isla gave Diego a cautious smile. She felt as though she'd held her own, but also that they had acted like a team. It was something she'd never felt with Kyle. There was exhilaration in the power of two. Even so...

"I would've preferred to work at the sanctuary."

Diego nodded. She saw that he understood, but that he wasn't going to budge on this point. Annoying as it was, she also felt that warm, glowing feeling that someone had her back. And not just any someone.

Diego.

If she didn't watch herself she'd go down the same path she had with her parents and Kyle. Seeking love and attention where it simply wasn't on tap.

"One step at a time, Isla. For now? You wanted to be useful and you will be. Consider yourself the victor. Maria del Mar is a force to be reckoned with."

"A force who would've preferred *she* was the one wearing this?" Isla held up her hand, shifting it until the diamond caught the light.

Diego nodded. "Perhaps. One day long ago." His eyes shifted to where Maria was disappearing around a corner. "She's married now. Happily, believe it or not. She generally just likes torturing people. I think it's a hospital administrator's mission."

Isla didn't press the point. There was clearly some sort of history there, but it wasn't as if *she'd* arrived on El Valderon with a clean slate. Well... it had been cleanish...slightly muddied...

Whatever. Her entire world was different now. *She* was different now.

To have gone from a sobbing-into-the-pillow wreck to a woman who could hold her own against another woman so obviously used to coming out on top of the food chain felt amazing. Maybe it was still adrenaline. Maybe it was the fact that she had no one here expecting her to be a particular way.

She stole a quick glance at Diego and fought the warm glow heating up her belly.

Maybe it was having someone believe in her.

She stepped away from the hand Diego was

about to put on the small of her back. "Why don't you show me the clinic?"

A few days later Isla's admiration for Diego had quadrupled. Every morning he ensured she spoke with her father via a video call, so they could each see the other was alive and well. The line usually broke up before either of them were able to say much, but it was ridiculously comforting to see her father in the little stone cottage. The same wee house he'd been raised in. But then once they'd changed into scrubs and climbed into the mobile clinic Diego treated her exactly as she'd been hoping he would: as a professional.

Seeing the island—Diego's homeland—this way also gave her a greater insight into the man who held her destiny in his hands.

He was generous. Almost to a fault. Kind. Patient. And he always had her safety in mind. She'd thought it would feel stifling...suffocating, even...to once again be filling a role she hadn't planned on: meek, over-grateful, reluctant, bride.

But it was quite the opposite. He expected nothing of the sort from her, and the feisty spirit she'd surprised herself by showing at the hospital that first day with Maria was something he not only enjoyed but encouraged.

This particularly bright morning he made the usual stop on their way out to the far end of the island and picked up Carmela's twenty-year-old granddaughter Sofia—"just in case the language barrier proves problematic".

It was his deft way of dealing with her minimal grasp of Spanish.

"Where is the next stop?" she asked. The mobile clinic had already stopped at a remote village and a tiny school.

"It's going to be a longer visit than the others. It's at the Vasquez Coffee Plantation."

"As in...?" She pointed at him.

He gave her a nod and a slow wink, which sent uninvited ripples of pleasure down her spine. She was going to have to find a tactful way to ask him to stop doing that. He was too...too *yummy* to also be flirty. This was work. She was *working*. Twenty-five more days and she'd be at home in the cottage, making her father hot chocolate.

A jag of discomfort blurred the vision.

Was that what she really wanted? To go back to the same old, same old? Had it ever been?

Diego, she abruptly realized, was merrily chatting on about the coffee plantation.

"It's a bit more diversified these days. When my father left and I had to take over the companies, I turned them into co-operatives. Fairtrade initiatives and the like. It's better for the workers that way. The co-operatives agreed to a pool of money going toward healthcare—which the hospital allowed to be used to fund the mobile clinic—and this way they can see, hands-on, that I care. And, of course…" he dropped her another of those steamy winks of his "…Maria isn't out of pocket."

Isla managed to ignore the wink and, because Sofia was clearly tuning in to their conversation, stemmed the questions she wanted to ask about his family and the businesses. Instead asked about the people they would be seeing.

"Poor, mostly. Laborers. They will likely never be rich." He sounded disappointed, but then regrouped. "They are certainly better off than they were when my father ran things."

"And he is…?" She left the question open.

"In Nicaragua. No doubt on his fourth or fifth wife and sixth or seventh business empire. Maybe both."

Diego kept his eyes glued to the road, his tone neutral, so Isla didn't press. She knew how complicated it could be to talk about parents. She still hadn't told Diego her own mother had died. That information felt like a precious secret that, if kept incredibly close and deeply private, might one day change the past.

A young girl's dream that would never come true.

After a few more minutes of driving in silence, he said, "My mother's in America. No doubt doing the same. With husbands. Not so sure about empires."

"I suppose everyone has their own way of dealing with grief."

"*Brava, cariña.* You're one of the few to see it that way. Most of the islanders think my parents are spoiled brats who left when the going got tough."

Isla looked out the window and swiped away an unexpected tear. "Let's just say my father didn't cope very well when my mother died."

Oops. So much for keeping her secret close and safe.

"Oh…?" he said simply.

It would have been so easy to pour out her life story. Tell him all the things she was sure he'd understand. How she'd become a doctor because it had been the one thing that might have helped her mother out there in the jungle. How she'd felt utterly powerless to keep her father safe, but loved him anyway. He was her *father.* How she'd become more and more conservative in order to counterbalance his recklessness. How she was wondering now if anything she'd done— her move back to Loch Craggen, her insane engagement to Kyle—had mattered.

Diego didn't press for more details, but he reached across and gave her leg a squeeze. He got it. Here was yet another layer of connection with this mysterious and wonderful man. She was really going to have to clamp down on her emotions if she was going to get through the remaining twenty-five days with her heart intact.

"Right!" Diego said eventually, pointing toward a huge wooden gateway that led down a beautifully manicured road to a series of low traditional stucco buildings. "Welcome to the plantation."

They parked up outside the cottages—which, he explained, were housing for the full-time workers. There was also housing further along the road, for people who had worked there their entire lives and were now retired.

"Like these houses? That's amazing."

He shrugged. "It's not much when you consider what their hard work has given my family."

And there he was in a nutshell. A man vividly aware of what he owed his community.

It didn't surprise her in the slightest when, just a few patients in, it became clear to see they adored him.

She'd never seen so many octogenarians fluttering their eyelashes, nor so much disappointment when they realized she was the one who would be taking their blood pressure.

"It'll be easier to get a more accurate read if you do it," he'd cheekily whispered in her ear as

one elderly woman blushed when he showed her
to a chair.

Isla had blushed too, when his hand had casually shifted from her waist to her hip, then lightly
grazed over the curve of her derriere as if they
had been married for years. Such a casual but
intimate gesture, and it was chased up by the
shock of realizing that the feeling she couldn't
put a name to when he dropped his hand was an
ache for more.

Diego was seeing their last patient—a teenage
boy—in the back exam room with Sofia when
a knock sounded at the open door. Isla took the
opportunity as a chance to try out her limited
grasp on Spanish.

"Adelante, por favor!"

A beautiful woman, exquisitely dressed with a
thick mane of black hair tumbling down her back,
stepped into the small waiting area. Isla pushed
her papers to the side of the table at which she'd
been working and half rose. They hadn't been
expecting anyone else.

The woman wasn't dressed at all like the other
women they'd seen. They had mostly been wearing thick cotton work clothes or brightly colored
traditional skirts and blouses. The fabric of this
woman's dress was clearly high quality. Raw
silk? A high-quality linen? The rings on her fin-

gers weren't cheap knock-offs, either. The sheer luster of them spoke of their authenticity.

She shot a nervous look behind her, then came and sat next to Isla at the table just outside another small exam room.

"How may I help you today?"

"You are Isla Vasquez?" The woman hesitated, a well of emotion clearly building in her throat.

Isla handed her a tissue. She'd always believed knowing it was safe to cry made it easier to stop fighting the emotion. When she looked at the woman's face again she saw tears brimming in her dark eyes.

"I am Serena Cruz."

For a moment the name didn't register. Then everything came together so rapidly Isla didn't have a moment to put on her game face.

Serena reached out and put a heavily jeweled hand on Isla's arm. "Don't be scared. I am here as a mother."

"Well, then…" Isla held her head high. "I will listen to you as the daughter of a man hounded away from a place he loved. At gunpoint."

Serena nodded, visibly taking on board what Isla had said. "I want to thank you."

For what, exactly? Surviving the most terrifying experience she'd ever been through? Agreeing to marry Diego to save her father's life?

She couldn't exactly spell any of that out. Diego had told Axl they were in love.

Then again, if Serena knew where she was— knew she was Diego's wife—surely she also knew this whole charade was a ruse to keep her father alive. A swirl of bile rose in her throat as she reminded herself that this woman's husband had threatened to kill her and her father. She owed her nothing. She pressed her lips tight.

"My son is alive because of you. And, of course, Diego."

Isla forced herself to speak levelly. "The way I understand it, *both* your sons are alive because of the Vasquez sons."

Serena shot her a sad smile. "This is true. But I believe it is you who has made the bravest of sacrifices."

Isla bridled. "I don't think so. I'm still alive." She let the words simmer between them, then softened. Serena obviously wasn't here to fight. "None of this needed to happen."

Serena shook her head. "When I met my husband he was a strong, honorable man. He worked hard. When the government changed in our country his job was taken from him. He lost himself that day."

Something twigged in Isla. Diego had mentioned earlier they'd be heading toward a village where quite a few Noche Blanca members lived, including Axl. He'd already been out this morning to change Paz's dressings, but had made no mention of seeing Serena.

"Does he know you're here?"

Serena shook her head, no.

"Why didn't you want him to know you were here?"

A tear lost its hold on Serena's eyelash and slid down her cheek. "I want my husband back. The man I married. I love him. And I will stand by him no matter what. Do you understand?"

Strangely, Isla did. It was exactly what she'd always done for her parents. Stood by them, all the while trusting, believing, loving. An invisible trinity holding her together through the darkest of days.

"Do you want out?"

Serena shook her head again. "No. But I want *change*. I know Diego is doing his best, but…"

"Everything all right in here?"

Isla's heart skipped a beat at the sound of Diego's voice. Her tummy did an entire tango when she turned around and saw him filling up the doorway, all dark-haired and pitch-black eyes… protective. Protective of *her*.

Serena rose and nodded solemnly at Diego. "Señor Vasquez."

He nodded, his expression inscrutable. "Serena. What brings you here? You know we planned on dropping by later."

"Si." She put on a neutral smile. "I was just extending my felicitations to your new wife."

Diego's eyes pinged to Isla. He didn't say anything. He didn't have to.

She held up her hands as if to say, *I'm fine. I will explain everything later.*

"How very kind of you." His voice was curt. Officious. "If that's all, then, we were just about to pack up and head out to Corona Beach. To see your son. The one with the gunshot wounds."

Diego knew he was pouring salt into a wound that would never heal. Knew Serena wasn't the one who should be on the receiving end of his verbal potshots. And, more than that, he didn't want Isla knowing there was this side to him. The side still seething with anger at the injustice of his brother's death.

Sure. He did his thing. He brought healthcare to the island as if he were a warrior and treating even the most vile of characters were his greatest pleasure. But seeing Serena here, on some sort of obvious power play with the woman he'd vowed to care for—that was stepping on territory he wasn't willing to give up.

He stepped to the side and showed her the door. "Do give Axl my very best."

Serena went to the doorway and then turned to him, nearly said something, reconsidered when he pushed himself up to his full height, and walked away.

After she'd gone he took two long-legged strides to where Isla was standing, her expression one of pure shell-shock.

He stroked her hair. Cupped her cheek. When he dropped his hands to her shoulders she shrugged herself away from him, visibly annoyed.

"Why were you so rude to her?"

"*Que*? *Cariña*, I was protecting you, not being rude."

She snorted. "Where I come from that sort of behavior is considered rude."

He *had* been rude. And a boor. And for the first time ever he liked having someone in his life who would hold his own actions up to him for examination. For too long he'd felt like a solitary crusader. A man hell-bent on bringing peace to the island through means he wasn't sure would ever wholly do the trick.

Isla crossed her arms and glared at him. He had to bite back a smile. Minute by minute she was slipping under his skin, and he didn't feel like putting up any sort of roadblocks to stop her.

"Do you know why she was here?"

"I would say to lord it over you, but I'm guessing by your reaction to my caveman routine I might be wrong."

"Correct. You're wrong. As my grandmother would say, you went a bit *crabbit* on the poor woman."

No guesses as to what *crabbit* meant.

He took a step closer toward her. "You know, you have a lovely way of rolling your Rs. Not everyone who tries Spanish can do that."

He took another step in and lightly rested his hands on her hips. She arched an imperious eyebrow at him, but didn't shake him off. He shouldn't be doing this. Neither of them should. And yet here they were. Neither of them moving.

Isla adopted an imperious tone. "I wasn't speaking Spanish. I was speaking Scots."

"And you and Serena were holding an international peace summit, I suppose?"

"As a matter of fact we were. Well… We might have been if *someone* hadn't showed her the door. I believe she was here offering herself as an olive branch, and if you hadn't come in like some sort of big old swashbuckling hero I might've found out exactly what it was she wanted."

Isla shifted under his touch and, if he wasn't mistaken, arched in toward him. Was she enjoying their feisty banter as much as he was?

Isla didn't blink. "Don't you believe me?"

"When it comes to you, my dear, I could

believe just about anything." He wove a hand through her thick hair and tilted her face up toward his. "But right now I'd like to talk about something else. In fact…" his voice lowered to a growl "…I'd like not to talk at all."

He closed the few inches between them, feeling the pulse of longing hit him fast and hard. Sofia had gone out. He kicked the door shut.

The minute his mouth touched hers, heat exploded in his body like a petrol bomb. Hot. Fast. Furious. It was as intense as their first kiss, but better. This time it was entirely by choice.

How did he know? He *felt* the difference. She'd responded to him before, but there had been so much adrenaline running through her system he hadn't been a hundred percent certain if she'd been expending her stores as a means of survival or acting on the same animal instinct that had made him kiss her in the first place.

This time he knew she was slaking the exact same hunger he'd been feeling from the moment he'd laid eyes on her.

She was tasting him. Touching him. Her hands were round his neck. In his hair. Rucking his shirt up and out of his trousers. Feeling his hot skin against her slender fingers. When she slid her hand between them and felt the strength of his desire they groaned together. He scooped her up and wrapped her legs round his waist faster than you could say—

"Oh! *Lo siento mucho!*"

They both turned to see Sofia, standing, frozen, in the open doorway.

Diego slowly eased his wife down his front, well aware that if he turned around he would be betraying more than elevated blood pressure.

"I— Should I—? Perhaps…should I go?" Sofia looked as if she wanted to run for the hills and never come back, but couldn't because her feet were cemented to the ground.

To his surprise, Isla slipped in front of Diego, pulling her scrubs back into a semblance of order, and smiled as if being caught in the throes of a passionate liaison happened to her all the time.

"Not at all. Apologies, Sofia. You'll have to forgive us…" She brandished her ring. "Newlyweds."

When Sofia made some sort of excuse about having left something a very exact "ten minutes away and ten minutes back", and slammed the door shut behind her, Isla whirled round and pointed her finger at Diego.

"No," she said, her chest still heaving, lips bruised, two bright dots of pink lighting up her cheeks. "No more of that. I'm *not* your property!"

He wanted to protest. Say he knew she wanted

him every bit as much as he wanted her, but demons of his own stepped to the fore.

Isla muddied his focus. His drive.

CHAPTER EIGHT

ISLA WAVED HER patient off, took the stethoscope from round her neck, popped it into her ears and pressed the diaphragm to her heart.

Ba-bump. Ba-bump.

Yup! Still beating. Would wonders never cease?

Clawing her way through these last few days pretending she was completely immune to Diego was an entirely brand-new form of torture. Particularly when patients asked about their plans. Did they have plans for the sanctuary? Remodeling? Were they taking a honeymoon? Starting a family?

It was the plans for a family part she found particularly difficult to grapple with. She really wanted children. When Kyle had left her, her very first thought had been, *Tick-tock, tick-tock.* It had been then that she'd known the rumored biological clock was very real. And painful to live with, considering Diego was so at ease with telling everyone, "The more the merrier!"

She'd never realized emotional torture could be physically painful before.

Life after that kiss...*those* kisses...all the fictions... *Sigh*. It would be an uphill battle to keep her strict, blinkered eyes on the actual prize—leaving El Valderon. Not to mention the fact that with each passing day the tension between the pair of them increased.

Pre-clinic kiss? Surprisingly light. Fun, even.

Post-clinic kiss? More...*guarded*. Intense. Driven.

It was almost impossible to figure out which one was the real Diego. Again and again she had to remind herself to fight her instinct to peel away the layers of this man who had unwittingly awoken something powerful and strong within her.

Today, in particular, as they worked at a remote mountaintop village school, Isla felt as though she were operating on a knife's edge—a totally different sensation from operating at gunpoint. This felt...insane, really. As if she'd been invaded by some sort of lust monster. A beautiful one. An Aphrodite. An insatiable she-devil. A *femme fatale*.

On a practical level, she knew she should be feeling fragile—terrified, even, given the fact her month in El Valderon was not even halfway done... But under Diego's gaze she felt empowered. Her entire body felt different.

Sure. She'd kissed other men before. She'd been intimate before. Felt the butterfly wing tickling of pleasure. But she'd never felt someone's unmasked desire invade her body like a nuclear-charged life force before.

"Isla?" Diego knocked on the doorframe of the tiny exam room where she was finishing up some paperwork.

He wasn't even touching her, and still...*fireworks*.

"Any chance I can borrow your lap?"

"I beg your pardon?" A rush of images jostled each other for pole position.

"For a child," he quickly explained, his expression neutral. "Sofia's nipped out. Would you be able to hold on to a four-year-old with some rather nasty splinters in her knee?"

"You need me to hold her?"

He tipped his head to the side, brow furrowed. "She's scared. Hurt. Her mother's not here, the teacher is busy, and I thought she could do with some comfort."

"But you're so good at that."

He shook his head. "Not with children."

"But I thought—"

"What?" An intensity she hadn't seen before radiated from him. "*What* did you think?"

"'The more the merrier?'"

Something bleak and painful darkened his eyes. "We tell people what they want to hear in public, *mija*. When it's just you and me I thought we'd opted for honesty."

Her heart sank. He didn't want children? Sure. On an intellectual level she understood why he couldn't have them right now, with her, but he was *great* with them. She'd seen him playing a game of hide and seek earlier and he'd been hilarious. Had had piles of children clambering all over him.

She rounded on herself. *This isn't about the two of you and your fictional future.*

"Isla? We need to get to my patient. Tick-tock."

Tick-tock.

"Of course."

She understood. It didn't sit well, but it wasn't as if having a real-life family was their destiny. She saw something in him relax. As if he'd been bearing the burden of his lies about wanting children on his own and now that she knew it was a burden halved.

"Right!" She stood up with as bright a smile as she could muster. "Let's go meet this little monkey."

A few minutes later Isla's every nerve-ending was at war with her common sense. Sitting there, in that tiny room, holding the most adorable little girl and watching Diego pull splinter after splinter after splinter from her knee…

It was like watching a man rescue kittens from a cliff-edge.

Utterly impossible not to go all gooey inside.

She let her cheek rest atop the little girl's head. It was so soft. For just a fraction of a second she allowed herself to wonder what it would be like if she was holding her own daughter, and Diego was the caring, loving father painstakingly extracting the remains of a log-jumping game gone wrong.

She lifted her gaze and met Diego's. He was looking directly at her.

Heat seared straight through to every part of her body it shouldn't. Every part of her body she had lectured each night about due diligence. An actual physical ache squeezed at her heart so tightly she could hardly breathe.

Was she falling in love with him? Her husband? Her captor?

He's not your captor. He saved you. And in two weeks he's going to let you go.

The flare of light in Diego's eyes was so intense she felt as if he was actually following her thoughts.

Just when she thought she couldn't bear it any longer, he dropped his gaze.

"*Ahora, mi muy linda niña.* That's you, all patched up." He lifted the little girl off Isla's lap and gave her head a little rub. "Let's let Isla go back to work now."

An electric tension simmered between them as Isla rose and left the room. It wasn't anger. Not loss. Or fear. It was sexual. Hot, fierce, sexual desire.

Two broken fingers, one mystery rash, three diabetes check-ups, four general health checks and about nineteen blood pressure checks on herself later, Isla and Diego called it a day.

When they got back to the house Carmela had already gone home.

The nanosecond the large wooden door to the courtyard shut behind her Diego became a man possessed. An explorer with one quest. One mission. To find the Holy Grail. And when Isla looked into his espresso-dark eyes, lit from within by the flame of desire, she knew without a shadow of a doubt that he'd found what he sought.

Without a word, he closed the space between them, reached out, took hold of the small waist tie that held her dress together and pulled it.

The woman she'd been a fortnight ago would have been horrified. The woman she was today felt beautiful enough to stand before him and let him appraise her.

She even shifted her leg, so that the wrap-around dress fell to the side, giving him more than a sliver of insight as to what lay beneath the fabric.

She didn't have to be told he liked what he saw.

His pupils dilated. His tongue swept across his lips.

Almost against her will, she did the same with her own dry lips, wondering if he could see the pulse-point at the base of her throat pounding. She dropped her eyes, half tempted to step forward and see how quickly she could make short shrift of the buttons on Diego's dark linen shirt, which accented the warm burnt sugar color of his skin.

Instead she let her gaze drop further. A warmth infused her entire body, coiling hot and tight between her legs as she saw the length of his erection appear instantly.

She'd never known the power of arousing a man just by standing in front of him. Seized with a boldness she'd not known she possessed, Isla slipped her dress off first one shoulder and then the other, catching the sleeves on her wrists, still keeping the whirl of fabric in place around her waist and legs.

He made a move toward her, his eyes glued to her breasts. Her nipples ached with need. For his touch. For his caresses. For the hot, wet licks she knew he'd give her with his tongue when she finally allowed him to come close and take her breast between his lips.

She shook her finger back and forth when he made a move to step forward. "Not yet."

"*Cariña*, you are torturing me."

"Isn't a new bride allowed to be shy?"

Where on earth had she found this new coquettishness…? She looked up to meet Diego's hungry gaze. Well… No guesses there, really.

She checked herself. It wasn't shyness. This was no ordinary margarita-fueled holiday romance. She wanted answers first.

"Is this real?"

A ragged breath left his chest and he held out his hands as if presenting his whole true self to her. "*Si amorcita*." He held out his wrists. "As real as what is flowing through these veins." He put his hands on his heart. "As real as what I felt the moment I first saw you."

"As real as this?" She held up her hand, showing him the ring he'd put on her finger.

Pain flashed across his eyes but he didn't blink. She knew it wasn't fair. Asking a man who'd married her in an insane situation to paint a picture. There wasn't a cell in her body that wanted to refuse him. That *could* refuse him. But she wanted to hear him tell her that what they were about to share was based on a fiction. That it *would* end. That anything and everything that passed between them was solely based on the here and now. Two hearts. Two minds. Two souls. One undeniably carnal attraction.

Diego stilled, then spoke, "The first woman who wore that ring—my grandmother—was the strongest, most noble woman I ever knew. She stood for truth, honesty and conviction. I vowed to her I would never put her ring on the finger of a woman who stood for anything less than she did. But as for what lies ahead for us...? I can make you no promises."

Isla respected his honesty. It wasn't as if she could, hand on heart, tell him she was in love with him. Did she care for him? Absolutely. Did she respect him. Beyond a shadow of a doubt. Did her body crave his touch?

More than anything.

She stared at the diamond ring on her finger.

She thought of her own grandmother, who had been her ballast during her childhood. With her parents constantly flying off to protect one endangered species or another Isla might easily have felt neglected. Uncared-for. But her grandmother had made sure Isla knew just how very much she was loved. From the look in his eyes, the ache in his voice, it was easy to see Diego's grandmother had been the same for him.

She didn't need to talk anymore. Quiz him. Push him into false declarations of feelings he couldn't possibly have. Not now. Not with so many questions left unanswered.

At this exact moment she wanted him. Plain and simple. The same way he wanted her.

She let her dress drop to the floor.

It had barely pooled round her ankles before she was in his arms, his mouth claiming hers more exquisitely than she would ever have imagined possible. His hands, broad and strong, spread along her back, her waist, her buttocks... all his touches and caresses leaving tendrils of heat in their wake.

As he drew her closer to him she reveled in the sensation of his shirt and trousers against her skin. The solid reminder of his ache for her. The warm, tropical air tickled like silk against her shoulders, between her thighs, on the soles of her feet as she went up on tiptoe to hungrily match his kisses.

Abruptly, he pulled back, his eyes burning with urgency and need. "You know this isn't real."

"This is." She put her hand on his pounding heart, then moved it to her own. "And this is."

"When this is over I will let you go."

She nodded. She knew.

"I'm not gone yet."

In one swift move, Diego scooped Isla up and into his arms and carried her toward the outside veranda—an enchanted sprawl of painted tiles, outdoor sofas and climbing plants, providing a private view of the sea and the setting sun just a few hundred meters beyond them.

Waves… The gentle shuffling of the palms… The shadow of the approaching moon… Apart from the elements they were completely isolated from everything and everyone.

It was his favorite place in the villa. Even more so now, as he watched his bride stretch out on the luxurious emerald and azure-colored cushions of the expansive daybed. He ripped the ties off the mosquito netting and watched as Isla disappeared behind the gentle billows of diaphanous curtains.

He stood at the end of the bed, open to the elements, and soaked in the vision that lay before him. She was dangerously beautiful, his wife. Her dark auburn hair fanned out against the pillows like rare silk, the sun's golden rays weaving through it for added luster. Her blue eyes were clearer than the sea behind him.

His gaze shifted to her kiss-bruised lips. To the pink on her cheeks that had come from the abrasion of his stubble. Fighting his desire for her had been like holding a savage beast at bay.

"I like it," she said.

"What?"

She pushed up on her elbows, the tips of her

nipples straining against the blue lace of her bra. "Your stubble. It's not as rough as you think."

He knelt at the end of the bed and began to crawl toward her, until he was straddling her, taking the bulk of his weight on his shins.

"Where would you like to feel it next?"

A wicked look lit up her features, her tongue dipping out of her mouth to lick her upper lip. "Surprise me."

His gut told him this was all new to Isla. The sensuality. The bravery. The brazenness of her longing. She was offering herself to him. And it wasn't in gratitude. It was because she wanted him every bit as much as he wanted her. So he was going to take his time and give her every ounce of pleasure she deserved.

"As you wish, *amorcita*."

He cupped her face with his hands and drew a long, sweet, hot kiss from her. There was an added boldness in her touch, different from just a few minutes ago when she'd dropped her dress and bared herself to him. She was wielding every bit as much power as he did, and she knew it.

They'd been open. Honest.

She was here now. And in a fortnight...as agreed...he would let her go.

"Unbutton my shirt."

She wriggled out from under him and knelt across him. She reached out, her fingers touching his lips. He drew them in to his mouth, his tongue swirling round them. Her other hand skimmed along the fabric barely containing her breasts, then down along her belly, then teased along the edges of her skimpy panties. Lava-strength heat harpooned straight between his legs.

"Forget it," he growled. "I can't wait that long."

He pulled his shirt off in one swift move. Her fingers reached out and found his belt buckle, undid it quickly then pulled it free of his trousers with whip-like precision.

Her hands sought his erection, straining against the fabric of his trousers, and stroked along the length of it. The rest of her body arched toward him as a little moan of pleasure swept past her lips. It was intensely erotic.

He clasped her wrists in one of his hands and pulled them up and over her head. He put his other hand to the small of her back. "Lie back. I want you to let me pleasure you."

"Not until you're naked," she whispered, undoing the buttons of his fly one excruciating button at a time.

It was his turn to groan.

The moment she reached the bottom button he yanked his trousers off, then stretched out along the length of her. Unable to wait for anymore commands he cupped one of her breasts while his mouth took the other through the delicate lace. Her fingernails bit into his back. He sucked harder, his teeth lightly grazing against her nipple, until he couldn't stand having anything between them. He flicked the clasp at the center of her chest apart and slipped the bra off, luxuriating in licking, sucking and kissing her breasts.

The more he touched her, the more her hips shifted and arched toward him. He gently grazed his hand along her belly, then slid it between her legs, where he could already feel she was ready for him. He slipped in a single finger, then another when she began to press against him with a rhythmic pulsing motion.

"I want you," she whispered into his ear as her hands raked the length of his back. "I want to feel you inside me."

He yanked his trousers up from the side of the bed and pulled out a small silver packet. He'd snagged a couple of condoms from the mobile clinic's supply after he and Isla had been caught kissing all those days ago. They'd been burning a hole in his wallet ever since. Now he wished he'd grabbed a dozen. More. The entire box might not be enough to sate his desire.

He quickly sheathed the length of his erection, then pulled her close to him, whispering again and again, "This is real."

Isla's entire body was humming with anticipation. She drew in a breath as Diego's arm muscles corded, taking the weight of his body as he held himself aloft. She had no actual control over her body's response to him. It was as if magnets had been placed inside her and were uncontrollably drawing her to him. Not that she wanted to resist.

He put a knee between her legs. "Wrap them round me."

His voice was so thick with emotion she felt tears spring to her eyes. A whimper of pleasure escaped her lips as she felt his length slide between her legs, shifting along the soft folds he'd already brought to a heated pool of readiness. Slowly, excruciatingly slowly, he began to slide into her. Teasingly. To the point where he knew she would have to beg. And she did. There was no shame in it. No weakness. Only pure, unadulterated need.

He drew out the long, heated strokes until neither of them could bear it anymore and she cried out for him to take her. His hips began to move with a more fluid cadence, faster, stronger, more demanding, until finally she knew he was no longer moving with control but with undiluted, animalistic need.

And then, as one, their hips met in one graceful, powerful connection and pleasure poured through her as they shared a mutual release. She clung to him, simultaneously exhausted and energized.

After a few moments he lowered himself, then rolled over onto his back, pulling her to him so that her whole body was stretched out along the pure masculine length of him. The sensuality of skin on skin—hers soft, his warm, hairy in parts, smooth in others—threatened to reignite the fire of desire all over again.

A soft breeze was shifting in from the sea, blowing along her back. She shivered—but not because she was cold.

Diego tightened his hold on her. "Everything all right, *amorcita*?"

"Mmm… More than."

She pressed a hand against his chest and pushed herself up so that she could see his face. For the first time he looked relaxed. Happy. Not a changed man, necessarily, but more…*complete*.

"Want to talk about it?"

She shook her head and drew her hand along the soft bristles of his five o'clock shadow. "No."

He let it drop, but she could see by the look in his eyes that he wouldn't forget. That she would have to find a way to tell him about how much he'd changed her. How when she'd arrived here she'd not only been a man's second choice, she'd become his reject. That the life she'd lived before meeting him had been a life crafted out of little more than fear. Fear of change. Fear of loss. Fear of being alone for the rest of her life.

And now she was halfway in love with a man who she would have to willingly walk away from if she wanted to live.

Diego reached up and swept a lock of hair behind her ear. "You look very thoughtful, *amorcita*. Are you sure you don't want to talk about anything?"

"I'm sure," she lied. "Just thinking about how this is absolutely the strangest holiday romance in the history of holiday romances."

His eyebrows nearly shot off his forehead. "Is that what you're calling this? A holiday romance?"

She shrugged. "No! I mean… What would *you* call it?"

She looked away, not really wanting an answer. They both knew what it was. A fiction.

Instead of answering, Diego wrapped his arms around her and pulled her to him, dropping a soft kiss on her forehead as the warm night air enveloped the pair of them in an invisible cocoon of togetherness.

Maybe she should stop asking questions, trying to define things, and give living in the moment a go.

She'd never lived her life as if she didn't have a care in the world, and in a strange way that was what her life was right here and now. Her father was at home. Safe. Her clinic was being covered by a really talented locum. Her ex, so she'd heard from her father, had applied for a transfer to "somewhere with a bit more pace" than Loch Craggen.

The only person she needed to worry about right now was herself, because for the first time in her life she felt as though someone truly had her back.

She pressed her fingertips into Diego's shoulders and nestled in close to him. Medicine, marriage and passion. It was almost unthinkably perfect...

But her heart nearly ripped at the seams as she let the truth invade it. This...the luxurious house, the extraordinary lovemaking, the undeniably noble man...none of it was based in reality. *Her* reality, at least. And sooner or later Isla would have to own the fact that everything that was happening between her and Diego was little more than a mirage.

She hid the tears that sprang to her eyes, nestling in even closer to Diego's warm chest, and made a promise to herself. She'd live in the moment. And when she walked away she would hold her head high.

CHAPTER NINE

EACH NIGHT SINCE they'd first made love they had shared the night together. Today, fresh back from a shift at the hospital, Diego pulled open the large, carved wooden door leading into the interior courtyard and burst into hysterics at the sight that greeted him.

Carmela had Isla up on the box she'd used to make him and his brother stand on when she was making clothes for them and had her draped in fabric every color of the rainbow.

Isla looked across at him, her eyes brightening as they met and, ironically or not, struck a pose akin to the Statue of Liberty. "What do you think?"

"I love it."

He gave Carmela an approving smile. The woman was clearly putting her stamp of approval almost literally on Diego's choice of bride. If only she knew the details...

He quietly harrumphed. Knowing Carmela, she *did* know the details. And now she was making a point. *Don't do what you always do and walk away. This one's a keeper.*

"So…" He tapped his index finger on his chin as he imagined a fashion designer might. "Is this an everyday outfit, or for something a bit more special?"

"Diego!" Isla gave her hair a coltish flick. "With you *every* day is special."

He wanted to believe it. Knew he couldn't. So he played along instead—just as she was. The pair of them assuming roles to make the best of an insane situation.

As mad as it was, he could genuinely see doing this for the rest of his life. Being caught in this bubble of happiness that surrounded the two of them, empowering them rather than breaking them.

He made a mark for Team Vasquez on his mental scorecard and put a large nil under Axl's. So far there had been no more trouble at the sanctuary. And no more mysterious "meet-and-greets" from Axl's wife Serena. That visit niggled, though. She'd never approached him before and, if it was true he had been as boorish as Isla had suggested, she might not again.

Had he missed a trick?

Proof, if he needed any, that letting himself fall for Isla would cloud his judgment.

"So?" He touched one of the fabrics—a luminous green. "What do you have in mind?"

Something flashed across her eyes he couldn't quite put a finger on. "Maybe when the dress is done we'll know what to do with it. For now I'd like to get back into my scrubs. Get word out about Phase Two of the mobile clinic."

"Phase Two?" This was news to him. "I didn't realize we had a Phase One in place?"

"Absolutely. Ooh!" She pulled a pin out of a piece of fabric held atop her shoulder and handed it to Carmela. In Spanish, she thanked her, then continued, "Is it all right if we finish this up tomorrow?"

"Absolutely, *señora*," Carmela cooed indulgently, throwing an unmistakable *I'm* her *housekeeper now* look at Diego. "Whatever you like. Shall I put dinner out for you at eight?"

Isla shook her head as Carmela began undraping the fabrics. "Don't worry. We can sort something out. Perhaps I'll make something Scottish for Diego. A bowl of Stovies? Or perhaps some clootie dumplings?"

Carmela gave her a dubious look, one that suggested nothing Scottish could match *her* cooking. It pleased Diego to see Isla laugh good-naturedly at the obvious slight. As if she were a part of the place.

She is *part of the place, idiota. You guaran-*

teed that when you put that ring on her finger. A
ring that saved her life.

"Right!" Isla rubbed her hands together once
her stint as a mannequin had finished and Carmela had disappeared into her sewing room.
"You ready to hear my plan? Perhaps over a glass
of wine out on the patio?"

"Sounds perfect." He dropped a kiss on to her
soft lips, instantly knowing, as she arched into
him, that a simple kiss wouldn't tide him over
until he held her in his arms tonight.

Skin against skin. Legs and arms tangled together. Hearts beating as one. He pulled her
closer to him and drew a long, sensual, heated
kiss from her not releasing her until he heard that
adorable little mew of happiness that meant they
either had to go straight to bed or stop touching
one another.

He pulled away. She wanted to talk. He owed
it to her to listen.

"Come, *amorcita*. Let's hear this plan of yours."

"So that's the plan in a nutshell."

Isla was unsurprised to see Diego's metaphori-
cal brake lights go on. The thing was, she needed
a project to distract herself from her looming departure date. She wanted to stay now, every bit as
much as she'd wanted to leave when Diego had
first slipped that wedding ring on to her finger.

And knowing that was going to require some serious distraction.

"There is no way she will go for it."

"But surely Maria will see the plus side of having a blood drive that would benefit the hospital?"

"*Sí,* but…"

"But what?"

He sat forward in his chair, elbows propped on his knees. "You want half the donations to go to the mobile clinic?"

She nodded.

"It's a great idea, but Maria would know that the blood would be going straight to Noche Blanca and would nix it in a minute."

"So if Noche Blanca were no longer a threat, *everyone* could receive healthcare?"

"Yes."

"Good. Then I think it's time we sat down with Axl Cruz and had a nice little chat."

"*Que?*" The brake lights went on again. "*Amor.* Things don't work so quickly here." He tapped his watch. "Island time. Besides, I thought we'd agreed to let things settle before we approached Axl."

She hung quote marks in the air with her fingers. "'*We*' agreed nothing of the sort. *You* made an executive decision."

"One that *you* agreed with."

Isla shook her finger in front of Diego's face and made a *No, I did not* sound. "There is no need for these ridiculous flares of violence. There's hasn't been so much as a whisper of crime in the past few weeks."

Diego's expression was deadly serious. "The incident at the sanctuary was huge. There's always a lull after that sort of things. People lay low. But it will happen again. Some would say it's human nature, *amor*. To fight. To have conflict."

"That's a pretty bleak attitude."

He fixed her with a solid gaze. One that reminded her he was a man who had lost his brother to violence. "There will never be a world without conflict. Without crime. Without loss."

It didn't mean they should give up. Just because they each bore the scars of other people's fury.

"I think peace *is* possible on El Valderon. *And* I think we should do a blood drive. Remind everyone they have the power to save lives."

He reached out and tucked a stray curl behind her ear. "How did one small Scottish island contain all this energy?"

She looked away. He wasn't to know she'd been an entirely different person less than a month ago. A person so intent on finding somewhere safe, somewhere it was impossible to get hurt, she'd not even noticed the only person she was hurting was herself.

Diego reached out a hand, sensing her change in mood, and pulled her to him on the deep sofa. She nestled in under his arm and pulled the other one around her, feeling his warmth as he cinched his fingers together and held her tight. She pushed away the mental reminders that none of this was real, because what she was feeling now was ridiculously real.

She loved him. She knew that now. Heart and soul. Loved everything they did together…

It was the type of relationship she was sure her parents had shared. One in which they'd stood up for what they'd believed in. Passionately followed their dreams. Their callings. It was an extraordinary privilege, she realized, to have grown up knowing two people who drew strength from one another to do what they thought was right.

She wanted to tell Diego *that* was the gift he had given to her when he'd slipped that ring on her finger. The gift of belief. Belief that she was strong. Capable of making change. Not just for herself, but for others.

"We'll talk to Maria."

He kissed the top of her head, and when he continued she could hear that same determined resolution in his voice she'd heard when he'd told her to marry him.

"It's time we shook things up around here."

She squeezed his hands tight, but didn't dare look at him. This was no holiday romance. Being married to Diego Vasquez was the most life-changing thing she would ever be a part of. And, even though it would only last a few more days, she renewed her vow to do everything in her power to help change the community he lived in for the better.

Maria was in full lioness mode. Diego took a step back, having learnt from experience that the best way to defuse her ire was to let her roar.

"The only reason I am agreeing to let you and the mobile clinic do it is because we don't have the staff to do a donation day. We need blood. Stores are low. But mark my words, Diego—" Maria pointed her painted talons at him, then Isla "—if people get even the slightest *sniff* that this blood might go to Noche Blanca…" Her dark eyes bored straight into Isla's as she continued. "They will never come."

Diego knew better than to step in and "protect" his wife. She could hold her own and *wanted* to.

Isla nodded, letting Maria know she'd heard her. "Your generosity will not be forgotten." She pressed a hand to her heart. "And this is a *good* thing. For the hospital. For El Valderon."

Maria sniffed, gave her a top-to-toe scan without moving anything other than her eyes. She pointed at the donors' chairs Isla had asked if they could borrow. "I want those back in pristine condition."

"Absolutely."

She gave them a curt nod, then swept out of the room.

When they were sure she was gone, Isla turned to him and did a melodramatic swipe of her brow. "Whew! She is a tough cookie."

"You're not wrong there. She's made of steel."

"And ice."

Diego tipped his head back and forth. It was more complicated than that. "She's...she's not just defending the hospital." He saw the dawning light of understanding hit Isla's blue eyes.

"She's defending her decision not to send the ambulance out for your brother?"

A grim smile served as his answer.

Isla scanned the morass of equipment. "Do you think this is madness? Moving all this gear on to the mobile clinic only for no one to come?"

Diego held out a hand to her. "We'll give it a few days so we can get the word out. The mere fact that Maria is so cross about it means she will be telling everyone. I'll tell Carmela, and all the people who work at the plantation. We're bound to have a few takers. At the very least we'll get the message out that the we need blood."

"*El Valderon* needs it. The *people* need it!"

She looked like *she* needed it. Was she pouring all her energies into work to keep her mind off the one-way ticket back to Scotland he'd booked the night before? He certainly was. Booking it had been his way of reminding himself this was all temporary.

"You're preaching to the converted, Isla. We have to take things as they come sometimes." He hoisted himself up onto the donor table and reached his hands out to her.

She didn't take them. She crossed her arms over her chest and said, "You're being defeatist."

Her words were like a searing hot poker plunged straight into a barely healed wound.

"Is *that* what you think? That I have given up? Is *that* why I arrived in the middle of the night to help Paz? Help you? Your father?"

Tears sprang to her eyes but Isla stood her ground, tilting her chin in that feisty way of hers. The way that indicated she was about to say something she knew would push the invisible envelope even more.

"How about I give Axl Cruz's wife a call? Serena? She seemed open to change. Given the blood you provided saved their son, you'd think they'd be keen to donate."

Diego shook his head and scrubbed a hand through his hair. "They won't come. Shouldn't come. Dodgy tattoos… Some of them might be users… Even if they could help, they never would."

"*You* show up. You show up whenever they need you, even though they took your brother." She held up her finger, where his grandmother's ring sparkled. "You helped a complete stranger. Why shouldn't they?"

"That's different," he deflected, trying to gather his thoughts.

"How? *How* is that different?" Isla pressed her hands to her heart. "Isn't it an innate instinct to help people?"

He shook his head, no. "I do what I do to make myself feel better. But the sad truth is it will never be enough. No matter how many blood drives we hold, or splinters we remove, or blood pressures we check, my brother will never come back."

Isla started to say something, then pressed her lips tight.

Diego felt an old idea resurface. The job offer he had made to Axl in the wake of his brother's death. The job Axl had refused. Perhaps enough time had passed to try again.

"We'll tell him about the blood drive. Axl."

"You will or I will?" Isla asked, her hands planted on her hips as she glared at him. When he didn't answer, she asked in a gentler tone. "What are we actually talking about here? Are we talking about bringing the people on your island together or ensuring they stay apart?"

And that was when it hit him. He'd been doing his absolute best to keep Noche Blanca away from everyone else. No one had gone to prison for what had happened to his brother. No one had had to do community service. *Nothing.* The only thing he had over them was the fact that they owed him. And by continuing to offer them medical care he was encouraging them to carry on with their "lifestyle choices."

He hopped off the donor table he'd been sitting on. "Leave it with me. I need to do this."

She shot him a dubious look.

He raised his hands. "I know. It's not like you don't have your own battles to fight with Axl. But mine…" He thumped his fist against his gut. "They live *here*. I'm asking you to trust me."

She quirked an eyebrow at him.

"I know." He put one of his hands on her shoulder, then tipped her chin up so that she could see straight into his heart. "I promise you I want the same thing you do."

"Well, then." She gave him an efficient little nod. "I guess you'd better get on with it."

After she had made sure absolutely everything was as organized as it could be, Isla pushed open the door. She was just about to unfurl the home-made signs she'd made when she looked out beyond the clinic's awning.

Her jaw dropped.

There was already a queue. Some thirty or forty people were standing outside the clinic, all waiting to donate blood. And the first ten were all people she recognized from Noche Blanca. Not the gang members themselves, but their mothers. Sisters. Cousins. Aunts. Uncles.

Her heart filled to bursting. Diego must have told Axl after all.

He'd been so quiet these last couple of days. So much so she hadn't even asked him whether or not he'd spoken to anyone, let alone Axl, about the blood drive. She had been so intent on distracting herself from her feelings for Diego, she was now worried she'd pushed too much.

The ring on her finger caught the morning sun. She'd have to return it soon. The sting of tears tore at her throat. She swallowed. Hard.

All good things must come to an end.

"Right everyone!" she called out in her fractured Spanish. "Let's do this for El Valderon!"

The crowd cheered and applauded. It was an extraordinary feeling. Being part of a place. Part of a movement for change.

When she turned around and saw Diego behind her, instinct took over. She went up on tiptoe and kissed him. "Thank you, Diego."

He whispered something in Spanish she didn't quite catch, but when he squeezed her hand and beckoned the people in the queue to enter, she knew the ties that already bound them had been strengthened.

CHAPTER TEN

"Right you are, my dear. I think that's you all bandaged up!" Isla smiled at ten-year-old Natalia, the young daughter of Gloria, who had worked for her father at the sanctuary.

The little girl had gone for a rather eventful swim with some of the baby sea turtles. She'd followed them all the way out to the reef and now had quite a deep cut on the top of her foot.

"Next time you go swimming do your best to avoid the coral reef, all right?"

Her eyes drifted to the beach. It was the first time she'd been to the sanctuary since the shooting. The blood drive had gone so well Diego had finally relented and let her unlock the gates to the beachside cove. They'd set up the clinic under a small copse of palms and had already seen a handful of people, including little Natalia.

"Do we need to do anything with Natalia's dressing? Change the bandages or anything?"

Gloria accepted the antibiotics Isla handed her. She had been in charge of the day-to-day running of the sanctuary since her father had left.

Isla shook her head. "Not for the next couple of days, Gloria. Unless she gets it wet. I know my dad—Doug—" She grimaced, then laughed. "It's weird talking about my father without him being here."

She waved away the unexpected rush of emotion that came with mentioning her father. *He's safe now.*

"Anyway. He would have helped you change the bandages. But we can do it here now. The antibiotics are precautionary more than anything. I wouldn't start her on them unless she begins to complain it's still hurting. It was a pretty bad cut, so it isn't always easy to rinse everything out, but we don't like to throw medicine at things that stand a chance of healing naturally."

"What kind of symptoms should I look for? If I need to give her the medicine?" Gloria pulled her daughter close to her side and popped a kiss atop her head.

The gesture was so simple. So natural. Casual, even. Yet it twisted Isla's heart so tight it nearly took her breath away. She didn't have memories of such gestures from her mother. Not that she hadn't been loving. She simply hadn't been there that often. To the point that when they had been together Isla had always felt a bit nervous about pushing herself on her mother. Appearing needy.

She often wondered if her mother and father had really thought the whole "let's have a baby" thing through. As much as it pained her to acknowledge it, both her parents' true love had been their work. Being at opposite ends of the earth had never seemed to bother them.

It was pointless drawing parallels, but every day she buzzed with the anticipation of seeing Diego on the days he worked at the hospital. In just a few short weeks he had shown her just how amazing a relationship could be...and their marriage wasn't even real!

The sex is real. The connection is real. The love you have for him is real.

"Isla? Are you all right?"

"Yes. Of course. Sorry. I went off to la-la land there for a minute, didn't I?"

She gave her cheeks a little pat and smiled apologetically at the pair of them. *How embarrassing.*

"What we're really looking to avoid is septicemia. So she should stay hydrated. Drink lots of water. Keep the wound clean. If it becomes inflamed, swollen or tender—those are signs there might be an infection. Spreading redness streaking out from the wound... If you want me to take a look at it again we're back..." She scanned the calendar she and Diego had drawn up a week earlier. "We're back on Tuesday. Two days from now."

Just a few short days before her flight.

Gloria looked over her shoulder, then leant close to her. "We want you to know the fact that you are here—that you and Mr. Vasquez have opened the gates and brought the clinic here—has given us the strength to carry on with our work. Change doesn't come easy. But we haven't given up on seeing your father's plans through."

Isla reached out and ruffled Natalia's hair. Protecting Natalia's future was precisely why her father had fought so hard to put those plans into place.

"How about when I come on Tuesday you and I set aside some time to talk?"

Gloria smiled and nodded. "That would be wonderful."

Isla made a couple of notes on Natalia's patient file, then went into the central reception area in the mobile clinic—which was, in truth, about five steps away from the table where she'd just been treating the little girl. In reality, the clinic it was little more than a glorified ambulance, but it did the trick. For them, anyway.

The night before she and Diego had made up a wish-list of things they'd like to change or add if they were ever able to get funding for a "proper" clinic. An extra exam room…an additional pair of hands, maybe. It hadn't hit her until now that what they had been doing was planning for the future.

A future she wasn't going to be a part of.

She stared at the door of the room where Diego was treating one of the guards who had been at the clinic *that* night.

Funny, she thought, how quickly she'd accepted this life, this lifestyle, as her own. Her eyes moved to the calendar on the wall. It had been exactly a month now. Her ticket was booked. Her carry-on bag lay on top of a chest, waiting to be packed. Shouldn't they be meeting with Axl? Discussing some sort of truce? Leaving with things so undecided seemed wrong.

Her stomach churned. And churned even faster when she heard Diego laugh with his patient through the thin walls.

She didn't want to go.

It was a life-altering revelation.

She didn't want to leave. Not Ei Valderon. Not the people they'd been helping. And most of all she didn't want to leave Diego.

As if on cue, he stepped through the door, shook hands with his patient, saw him out, then crossed to her and kissed her cheek.

"Everything all right, *mi amor*?"

The term of affection did the same thing it did every time Diego used it when he checked in with Isla. She smiled as she tried to neutralize the fireworks going off in her belly, the skip of her heart.

She smiled up at him. "All good."

He pulled his laptop onto the counter and started to make some notes, then looked up when he noticed she was still looking at him. "What do you say we have dinner in town tonight? Somewhere special?"

She hadn't been feeling a hundred percent that morning, but he looked so keen. "Any particular reason?"

He feigned mock horror. "It's our one-month anniversary, *amorcita*. We can't let the good people of El Valderon think I am not still treating you like a *princessa*."

She smiled, but the comment hurt more than it salved her already jangly nerves. He was still playing a role. The lovestruck doctor in a whirlwind romance.

A *fake* whirlwind romance that had saved her life.

She had to admit she had put down half of the nerves and the churning in her stomach she'd felt lately to her increasing anxiety about when her path might cross with Axl Cruz's again. Would the invisible stranglehold he had on her life drop away? With Diego she felt safe. But when she was home again in Craggen…would the fear return in force?

Another thought struck so powerfully she felt numb.

What if this "date" tonight—this public show of affection—was actually Diego's way of telling the island it was over?

She looked at Diego, at his strong profile, his kind eyes… Would he really do that? Shame her in the same way Kyle had?

No. Not the Diego she knew. He wouldn't do that. Couldn't. Unless this whole time she had been the unwitting pawn in a much bigger game. A game to outwit Axl Cruz.

She was just about to ask Diego if they could go to see Axl—find him, hash out what had actually happened—when there was a knock at the clinic door.

Sofia.

Isla smiled across at the young woman who had become a real asset for the mobile clinic. Not to mention a bit more wary about entering the clinic unannounced since that day when Isla had been so steamed up by Diego's kisses she hadn't even bothered with feeling embarrassed.

"Are you ready for your next patient?"

"Absolutely." Diego rubbed his hands together. "Who do we have next?"

Sofia winced at him. "Paz Cruz."

"Ah." Diego drew his brows together, as if the news had caught him by surprise. When he noticed Isla staring at him, he gave her a quick smile. "Good. Nice to see he's up and about."

"Not at my father's sanctuary, it isn't."

Everyone stared at her.

Diego stepped between her and the doorframe, giving a quick signal to Sofia to stall Paz.

"You've seen him recently, haven't you?" Isla stood and crossed her arms. She could see by the shift of his eyes he knew she didn't mean Paz. She meant Axl.

"*Amor…* I haven't seen him. No one has."

She doubted that. Part of Diego's strength of character was his unerring quest to keep her safe and out of the reach of Axl Cruz.

Well, being kept in the dark wasn't good enough. She was going to have to get used to looking after herself soon enough, so why not start now?

She stared at Diego, a mixture of frustration, betrayal and love gnawing a raw black hole in her belly.

How could she have let herself fall in love?

"Fine." She squared herself off to Diego. "Compromise. If you won't tell me what you and Axl have been up to, let me treat Paz. If he's actually here for an appointment."

She wanted to look the man in the eye—the

man whose life she'd helped save. See if he knew how much pain he'd caused her father.

Their daily video calls were…*complicated.* Her father would pass on reams of instructions, she'd pass them on to Gloria… But until today, when they'd finally felt it was safe to open the sanctuary, she'd been completely powerless to help.

Diego shook his head. "That won't be necessary."

"I think it will." She gave him her best *I'm not going to budge* smile. If she was going to leave this island with a broken heart, she was also going to leave it with her head held high.

"Different compromise," Diego parried, taking a step closer toward her.

Which was clever. He knew she got all wobbly-kneed the closer he was.

Her pulse quickened as she waited for this alternative compromise.

"We do it together."

She pretended to consider it and saw from the smile teasing at the corners of his mouth that he knew damn well she was vulnerable to that cheeky smile of his. This man… There was no staying cross with someone who made her laugh, made her feel protected, not to mention feel as if she were the only woman in the world he wanted to hold in his arms.

Even if it was all a lie.

Tick-tock.

"Right, then." She peeled her eyes away from his. "Let's see Paz."

"It looks good." Isla took out some fresh bandages. "No swelling. No discharge. You've clearly been taking care of it."

Paz nodded. He hadn't said more than two words since he'd entered the exam room with the pair of them.

Diego gave Isla a sidelong look. One that was trying to gauge if she was irritated because he was there or irritated because of their patient.

Easy enough to see she wished he would leave. *Tough.* They'd made a deal. The fact he'd insisted upon being there was... Well, he'd hoped it would be more reassuring than annoying. There wasn't a chance in hell he was going to let Isla be hurt. Not tonight. Not ever again.

This isn't a forever game.

A weight landed in his gut.

It wasn't a game at all.

He needed to talk with Axl. Clear the path for Isla to go home.

Don't let her go. Tell her how you feel.

A buzzing began in his ears. That was precisely the problem. He didn't *know* how he felt. Teasing away fact from fiction had proved too difficult. The only thing he knew was real was how perfect it felt to hold her in his arms. How well they worked together. How, as a team, he felt they could conquer anything they wanted to.

He looked at Isla, wondering if she felt the same. From the face of it, it was impossible to tell. She was a picture of concentration.

"It looks like the Steristrips have all done their jobs. Did they naturally disintegrate or did you take them off?"

Paz muttered something he couldn't quite make out. Diego could tell the lad was uncomfortable. Whether it was because of Isla's presence or his was unclear.

"I know you've met with my husband a couple of times since you received your injury." She nodded toward Diego, but didn't meet his eyes. "How did those appointments go?"

Again, Paz muttered something largely unintelligible. No overt thanks, but neither was there any hostility. Or bravura. One might easily have imagined him swaggering in here, making threats, showing his strength—*his* father had bullied Isla's father out of the country.

"You were lucky. This could have been much worse. I believe my father was always pretty clear with Security that if things ever turned violent he would prefer they not make full use of their marksman skills."

Paz shot her a look.

"You probably already know this, seeing as it's such a small island, but all the security guards here are ex-military. Men who know the true value of life."

Diego was about to jump in, smooth things over, but Paz wasn't bridling as he thought. Perhaps he could see what it was he hoped Isla was doing. Showing Paz the same amount of respect they had shown him and his family.

They'd saved his life. His own government had refused to do the same. Fair enough that she would want some common courtesy in exchange. She would be such an asset to the island's community. A true role model.

What's stopping you from asking her to stay?

"I presume Dr. Vasquez has already given you a timeline, but I expect we'll be able to take these staples out in the next week or so." Not that she would be here. "We wouldn't want them leaving any permanent marks, would we?"

"My father's dead."

Diego did a double-take.

Isla looked just as shocked.

"What did you say?" Diego asked.

"Axl. My father. He was killed three days ago, on an island off of the coast of El Salvador."

"What was he—?"

Isla's question remained unanswered as she

and Diego silently listened to Paz explain how Axl had left El Valderon on the off-chance that Isla called the police or Interpol. When he'd arrived on a new island he'd tried to establish his authority in a place that had zero tolerance for *pandilleros*.

Axl Cruz was dead.

"I want out," Paz said now. "I don't want to fill his shoes." He met their astonished faces head-on, shoulders back, eyes unblinking. "You saved my life." He held up his hands as they both began to throw questions at him. "I want to honor the sacrifices you've made in your lives by changing mine."

Tears sprang to Isla's eyes. "Do you…do you have a plan or—?"

Diego cut in, putting a hand on his wife's back in a form of apology. This was game-changing stuff. The son of the island's terrorist was doing an about-face and choosing peace.

"Does your mother know about this? Have you told her anything?"

Paz looked away, then back at the pair of them.

It struck Diego that the young man was addressing them as a couple. He hadn't seen them being married at gunpoint. Hadn't seen the fear in Isla's eyes when Axl had threatened to kill her and her father. He'd only known them to be two people brave enough to step between warring factions and save his life.

A bolt of understanding hit him with lightning-strike precision.

He hadn't cared about putting himself in the line of fire before because he hadn't seen any reason to preserve his own life. Did he have a death wish? No. But did he have a reason to live?

He looked at the woman who stood beside him. Fierce. Brave. Compassionate. Loving.

Yes. Yes, he did.

Dr. and Dr. Vasquez. A married couple. A couple who served their community the only way they knew how: *together*.

He channeled the man he wished his father had become when their lives had been torn apart after Nico's death. A man who absorbed grief and turned it into good. Genuine, goalless good.

"What do you want, Paz? How do you see yourself changing?"

"I want to study medicine."

Isla looked across at Diego. He saw she was thinking the same thing. This was clearly a turning point and they would be fools to let any momentum they'd gained fade away.

He heard commitment in Paz's voice. Strength. He saw the change in his body. A different type of voltage fuelling his path in life.

Diego was also feeling a fresh surge of energy.

The same invigorating charge he'd felt the night he'd pulled his grandmother's ring from his neck and slipped it on to Isla's finger.

It was the energy of change.

Paz was clearly expecting to be laughed at. Mocked. Turned away. Instead Diego took his declaration seriously. He pulled up a stool and sat across from him. Eye to eye. Man to man. He sat taller when Isla came up behind him and swept her hand along his shoulders. They were a team now. An indivisible team.

"You'll have to go away to study if you want to become a doctor. The university here isn't equipped for anything beyond nursing degrees or emergency medicine for paramedics. You can go to the States or…elsewhere."

He pointed vaguely in the direction of Latin America. He began talking to Paz about school options, the courses he'd have to take, the subjects he'd need to study to put himself on track for a medical degree.

The young man was like a sponge. Absorbing it all. Asking questions. He was completely engaged in finding the best way to make his decision. The *right* decision.

"At that point you'll have to choose a discipline…" Diego pulled out a blank piece of paper and started writing lists.

Isla gave him a nudge with her elbow. "The poor man's eyes are glazing over!"

"It's a big decision. He needs all the information."

"True…" She drummed her fingers along her mouth.

Heat shunted through him at the memory of her hands on his body, her mouth kissing his. Each night they shared together was better than the last. The memory of those sensations was so powerful it took him a moment to tune back in when she started speaking.

"…an idea I think could work."

They both looked at her, a bit shocked as she had been so quiet before.

"Diego, you're working at the hospital these next few days, right? The accident and emergency ward?"

"*Sí*…" He drew out the word, unsure as to where this was going.

"That means I'll be on my own. So…why don't we park the mobile clinic up here at the sanctuary on a more permanent basis? It's near the villages, easy to get to. Paz can help me make it a sanctuary for people as well as turtles. I'm in if you are."

She put out a hand to shake on it.

Paz stared at it.

It was a big ask.

Everyone in the room knew it.

It would tell the island that they were united in their mission for peace.

"You want me to come *here*?" Paz sounded utterly flabbergasted. "To the sanctuary?"

Diego couldn't stay out of the discussion any further. "I don't know if it's wise, *amorcita*."

He knew his body language was defensive. Protective. Only this time he wondered if what he was really protecting was the status quo.

"If my father can't be here," Isla said, "*I* want to be here. And who better to make this place a genuine sanctuary for the islanders than Paz?"

There were about a thousand different options he could offer here, but Diego was struck by the fire of possibility brightening his wife's eyes.

She crossed her arms and gave Paz a solid look. "I presume you won't be advertising free turtle eggs to your friends?"

He had the grace to look ashamed.

Isla pulled up the other stool so they were all sitting at the same eye level. Paz had obviously come here in good faith. He was trusting them. Isla was trying to do the same.

"What does your mother think about you being here?"

"She's the one who told me you might be able to help."

He was looking directly at Isla. The penny dropped.

This was why Serena had come to the clinic the other day. They *both* wanted change. *They* were frightened of Axl...or at least of who he'd become. And they'd been brave enough to ask for help.

"Do you think you being here on a daily basis, helping with the clinic, will provoke the other members of Noche Blanca?" Isla asked.

The question was a serious one. There was no chance this would work if it would bring more violence.

Paz looked them both solidly in the eye, "Without my father there *is* no Noche Blanca."

"Right, then." Isla gave Paz's arm a squeeze. "I'll see you here tomorrow. If you like we can get you some scrubs to wear. Make you look like part of the team."

She and Diego both smiled as Paz's eyes lit up. "Really? I can wear scrubs? That would be amazing! It'll be just like on TV."

"Better than TV," Isla corrected. "You will be helping real people in your community."

Diego watched his wife say her goodbyes to Paz with a warm hug and that big, beautiful smile of hers.

Just for that perfect moment he let himself believe it was all real. That they were a real married couple, making changes in their community step by proud step. And, just for that instant in time, he felt as if he could leave his anger from the past behind and face the future with a smile. With hope.

CHAPTER ELEVEN

DIEGO THANKED THE waiter for the nibbles and gave Isla's hand a squeeze. "Help yourself, *amor*. The meal shouldn't be too long." He popped a few salted peanuts into his mouth and then, after they'd both enjoyed the setting sun for a few moments, said, "I have to admit I'm still a bit shell-shocked."

"About Paz wanting to work with us? Or about his father?"

They'd each had a few hours to process and confirm the news. Axl Cruz was dead. For Isla it changed everything. She could go home now if she wanted to. Or, if she *really* wanted to drag her heart through the coals, she could wait until her father's inevitable return.

He'd not want to stay in Craggen anymore. Not now that he was free to work at the sanctuary again.

She watched as Diego's features softened into a philosophical expression. With every fiber of her being she would miss this man.

"I'm not surprised about Axl. Relieved, in a

way. Saddened that he never had to stand up in front of a court of law, but to have Paz come forward the way he did… *Amazing*."

He started to drop her one of those winks she had expressly forbidden, then stopped himself.

"I think it's a real credit to you that he chose you to work with."

She bit her lip. Why was he pretending it was going to be for anything more than a handful of days? Her plane ticket was booked.

"He'll learn every bit as much from you."

Diego reached across and squeezed her hand, then drew it to his lips and kissed it. Warm fuzzies blurred any lucid thoughts she might have had about how her leaving now was actually a *good* thing.

"What do you mean?"

"I'll be off soon, won't I?"

She said it casually enough, but the air between them grew taut with tension.

Diego's eyes told her everything she needed to know. He was ready for it. Ready for her to go.

Which was why it came as a complete shock when he said, "You could extend your stay. For a while."

And there it was. The final nail in the coffin.

She needed to go home. The sooner the better. Prolonging this agony of a love that was so obviously unrequited…it was too painful. Besides, Diego might have made huge strides toward making peace with his own demons, but being here had allowed her to push hers into a cupboard and do her best to forget about them. Disguise them with the adrenaline rush of survival. Of falling in love.

"Before I came here…" Her hands began to shake at the flood of powerful memories, so she set down her fork. "Before I came here I was engaged to someone else."

If she hadn't had Diego's full attention before she had it in triplicate now.

"And you ended it?"

"No. Quite the opposite. He chose another woman over me."

"Obviously the man is an imbecile."

She wanted to say, *Yes. Absolutely. A liar and a cheat.* Those were the facts. But the reality was she couldn't let Kyle bear the brunt of the responsibility that the clarity of hindsight inevitably allowed.

Instead, she said, "I probably owe him a thank-you card, to be honest."

"Que?"

She drew little gratification from Diego's indignation.

"Seriously. I could throw him to the lions, but…but I was probably every bit as responsible for the relationship being a disaster as he was."

"If anyone should thank him for being such a fool it should be me. I won the bride."

She shook her head. "No, you didn't. Axl did. Fear did."

"You think fear was what made you say yes? Go through with the marriage?"

She nodded. "Of course it was! I was fearing for my life. My father's life."

As she spoke, the memory of how she had really felt shunted through her every bit as powerfully as if she were reliving it.

"*Cariña...*" Diego protested. "Only a woman shot through with *bravery* would have done what you did."

She fought the bloom of warmth and strength his compliment elicited. "There was some courage involved. Courage I wouldn't have felt if it hadn't been for you." She hesitated. "I *should* thank Kyle, though. I went back to Loch Craggen after my mum died because I thought if I had the perfect job, the perfect family, gave my father grandchildren..." She paused only just catching Diego's infinitesimally small flinch. "Like an idiot I thought grandchildren would be enough to make my father come home. Now that I've seen him here I realize he's doing what he loves. That he wasn't built for traditional parenting...whatever *that* is. So, yes. I do owe Kyle a thank-you."

"For what? Making sure you didn't have children?"

"No!" she snapped, a bit more grumpily than she'd intended. "For forcing me into a place so vulnerable I only had two choices."

"What were they?"

"To fight or to give in. Turns out fighting is a whole lot more rewarding."

And a crucial reminder of why she so longed to stay. She'd taken to this lifestyle. To these people. To Diego. She hadn't told him, but her locum had expressed an interest in staying on in Craggen for longer. Her father seemed different too. He seemed to have... Well, he seemed to have bloomed a little, and was spending quite a bit of time with Mary Baird.

She took a drink of water to give herself time to gather her thoughts. "Have I ever told you how my mother died?"

"Not in so many words."

As the sting of tears hit, Isla was suddenly grateful for the isolated table Diego had requested for them, out on the seaside patio. She was normally much better at controlling her emotions, but—*tick-tock*. She wasn't going to be here much longer. She might as well leave Diego with a full portrait of the woman he'd risked his neck for.

The woman he was rejecting.

She swiped at the tear careering down her cheek.

He pulled out a clean handkerchief and handed it to her with a gentle smile. The simple gesture tore at the fragile hold she had on her emotions. She stemmed a small sob, then buried her face in the handkerchief that smelt so perfectly of him until she could speak like a vaguely normal human being.

"For as long as I could remember my parents were devoted to saving animals as much as they were devoted to each other."

"And to you?"

She swallowed back the urge to tell him they had never loved her as much, but that wasn't true.

"I don't think they were designed to be stay-at-home parents. I know they loved me, but they saw their causes as bigger than them. More powerful."

A rueful smile hit Diego's lips. "I can relate."

"And because of that," Isla continued, "you've helped me understand my parents more. Helped me realize they did love me, with all their hearts, but the *way* they loved me was always going to differ from the way people who 'toe the line' love."

"How do you mean?"

"My mother was killed trying to protect a young assistant and an orangutan. Poachers. They were armed. She wasn't. The assistant was trying to protect the orangutan…my mother intercepted the volley of bullets.

Diego winced. He now understood just how similar their paths had been. But his response to tragedy had been so much more proactive than her own.

"When my father left his elephant project—"

Diego's eyes widened.

"I know, I know… There are a lot of endangered species. From my perspective, seeing as I'd already lost one parent, I felt I in danger of losing another. So I upped sticks and did everything in my power to make myself into a safe haven for him, back in my grandmother's house on Loch Craggen. But really I was making it a safe haven for *me*. Cocooning myself against all the scary things. I dropped my exciting life in London like it was burning coals. Took over the GP practice. Helped elderly ladies across the street. Drank hot chocolate instead of wine…"

"Became engaged to someone you didn't love?"

She gave him a grim smile. "Yup. And I hung around long enough for him to get bored with this…" she drew her hands along the length of her body "…and ended up here, sobbing myself to sleep every night until…until I met you."

"Why are you telling me all this? Not that I

don't want to hear it… It's just that you've had all month to explain."

She was telling him because she loved him. Because she wanted him to know that as she confessed to him it was coming from a place that was honest and true. But she didn't think he'd want to hear that. Not if his invitation for her to stay was only "for a while."

She forced herself to give a self-effacing laugh. "I guess it's a really long-winded way of telling you that you're the one I really owe thanks to."

"I think you could safely say the feeling is mutual. Now!" He looked at the steaming plates of food the waiter had just set down between them. "Shall we enjoy our meal and then…" he dropped her a sexy wink "…have an early night?"

The warmth in her chest turned to fire. A fire that arrowed down to her body's most intimate regions. She hardly needed to be told what her body wanted. What she did need was for her brain to come to terms with the fact she would have to say goodbye.

"Absolutely. *Bon appetit.*"

She speared a prawn with her fork and raised it to her lips. The instant the scent hit her a swell of nausea roiled in her belly.

She looked up at Diego. Their eyes met with an electric, unbreakable connection as the fork fell from her fingers and her hands flew to her mouth.

In that instant she knew exactly why her body was behaving this way. The easy tears. The zig-zagging emotions. The nausea.

Despite their precautions, despite the fiction of their marriage, and despite playing their emotional cards as close to their chests as possible… she was carrying his very real child.

CHAPTER TWELVE

THERE WAS ONLY so much pretending Diego was up to. Isla had been in a dark mood ever since her bout of food poisoning.

"Everything all right?"

"Yes, thanks." She took a sip of herbal tea instead of her usual coffee.

He didn't like this. Pretending they were a couple who barely knew one another instead of a couple who had shared a bed up until a week ago. Shared a bed in a rather spectacular fashion.

He scalded his throat, downing his morning coffee in one, his eyes glued to his wife. "Do you want to talk about it?"

"Nothing to talk about."

It was the same line she'd used for the past two days. And tonight she would board a plane for Scotland.

She was proactively avoiding any and all conversations that didn't involve the clinic. Nor had she slept in his room. The gesture felt like a knife blade searing directly into Diego's soul. He wanted to push. He wanted to demand. He wanted, he realized with a burning hot resolve, this marriage to be real.

But she'd very obviously turned some sort of corner and was set on going home. He could hardly demand she stay. Not after everything she'd been through.

He nudged the basket of baked goods toward her. "*Amor*... Try something. A bit of bread? You've hardly eaten all week."

He saw her fight a swell of nausea.

"Still not feeling well?"

She shook her head. "I have to get to the clinic soon. I'll eat something at the sanctuary."

"Why are you going to work? You're leaving tonight."

"I don't really need reminding, Diego," she snapped.

Fine. He'd try another tack. "Is Paz working with you today?"

She screwed her lips up for a minute and thought. "Yesterday was Sofia, so today is Paz."

"He seems to be taking to his volunteer role like a duck to water."

She smiled, despite the obvious discomfort she was feeling. Whether it was still the nausea or his presence remained to be seen.

"I can't yet tell if he simply likes wearing scrubs or if he's really taking to medicine."

"Maybe a bit of both?" Diego suggested.

She shrugged and looked away.

"Have you spoken with your father?"

"No." Her hands swept to her belly. "I... I send him emails. We're in touch, but..."

Diego reached across and took Isla's hand in his. "*Amor*. Talk to me. None of this is under duress anymore. I'm here. For *you*."

Tears sprang to her eyes. She pressed her lips together, fighting the emotion he could see clawing at her throat.

"We can get through this—whatever it is. Together."

"That's just it!" The words came out in a torrent. "We aren't a *we*. Are we?"

She opened her arms wide and scanned the sunny courtyard where they'd taken their breakfast so happily for the previous few weeks.

The thought sickened him.

The idea of living without Isla was even worse.

"We can be if you want to be."

She looked at him as if he'd just spat at her. Her features twisted in horror. "What? Live a lie? Tell our child—?" She choked on the word, her hands pressing protectively to her belly.

He stopped her. "*What* did you say?"

"I said our child." She lifted up her chin. Defiance was pouring from her.

"You're pregnant?"

He felt as if he'd been hit with a wrecking ball.

His vow never to have children was the one thing he had never questioned. The one vow he'd always believed he would keep.

"I wasn't going to tell you. I was trying to keep the little bubble of this lie we've been living complete so that you never had to know."

Diego bridled. "Is that what you think? That everything we've been through is a lie?"

"What would you call a marriage at gunpoint?"

"Love at first sight," he answered, without pausing to think.

They stared at one another, absorbing the power of the words he'd just spoken.

"Is that what you genuinely feel?" she asked eventually. "Love? Are you sure it's not some Messiah complex? A built-in need to protect vulnerable people after your brother died?"

He stared at her and said nothing. An instant ago, when he'd said "love at first sight", he'd believed it to be completely true. He'd been bowled over by her from the instant he'd laid eyes on her. Instinctually drawn to protect her. Care for her. Ensure she was—

Hell. She was right. He had been protecting her. But did he *love* her?

It was impossible to know. How did a man go about teasing apart fact from fiction?

He was surprised to see she was pushing back

from the table—away from him. "The fact you're not answering is giving me your answer."

"Isla, wait."

"No." She shook her head and held out a hand in a *stay where you are* gesture. "I don't want you treating me as if I'm weak. Or vulnerable."

She looked up at the sky, blinked away a couple of tears, then met his gaze head-on.

"What I am is strong. Resilient." She pressed her hands to her heart. "I know now I'm a survivor. I don't need you to protect me. Or care for me. Or create some sort of cocoon for me to live in. Because loving you has changed me."

Her sob echoed around the sunlit courtyard as she dropped her face into her hands.

She loved him?

Instinct drew him to her. He pushed his chair back and tried to pull her into his arms but she pushed him away.

"I don't want this. I don't want you if you don't love me."

Why can't you just tell her? Tell her how you feel?

He scrubbed his hands through his hair. "We've got quite a few questions up in the air, don't we?"

She made a noise in her throat that told him what he already knew. That he was prevaricating. Being pathetic.

Loving her doesn't have to mean losing her. She's not your brother. This is not the same scenario.

"Isla." He reached out as she passed and grabbed her wrist. "If you're carrying my child—"

"Stop! Stop trying to control the situation. I gave myself to you. Heart and soul. Willingly. Do you how painful it is for me to know you won't do the same?" She turned on him. "You don't even want children, Diego. You made that crystal-clear. *I do.* So do what you do best and leave me to get on with my life!"

He reached out and grabbed her wrist. Things weren't going to end this way. Not with a fight.

She yanked her wrist out of his hand. "Don't!" She massaged her wrist and stared at him, appalled. "Don't you *dare* try and stop me."

She headed for the stairs then turned on him again.

"Do you know how much trust it took for me to fall in love with you? How much faith? To convince myself you weren't like *them*? That you were kind? Good? Someone who was doing his best to rise above and make a difference? Well, it turns out you're just like my parents. You love the cause much more than the people involved in it. I *won't* be a victim of that again."

Then she ran up the stairs and into her room, where it didn't take a genius to figure out she would be packing her bag and preparing to leave.

CHAPTER THIRTEEN

A KNOCK SOUNDED at Isla's childhood bedroom door. "Hot chocolate, love?"

Isla shook her head. "No, thanks, Mary. I'm all right with mint tea for now."

She held up the mug sitting on her bedside table as if it was proof that mint tea was the thing she most wished for in life. The magic potion that was making everything about being back in Loch Craggen pregnant, alone, and living under the same roof as her father and—*hello!*—his new girlfriend completely natural.

"How're you getting on with the job-hunt?" Mary leant against the door, clearly not planning on budging until she got an answer.

Isla smiled at her persistence. No wonder her father was cock-a-hoop over this woman. She was strong. Emotionally grounded. As mad about dogs and Craggen as he was about turtles. And she never pushed Isla to talk more than she wanted to.

"Well…" Isla pushed aside her laptop and crossed her legs. "I have applied for four posts in London, but being two months pregnant isn't really much of a lure to prospective employers."

"You're a sensible girl. You have savings. And of course your father and I are happy for you to stay here as long as you like."

She didn't want to stay here. She wanted to go back to El Valderon, where her father was on a quick advisory trip. He'd handed over the reins of the sanctuary to Gloria, with the tacit agreement that he would come out during egg-laying and hatching season each year.

It was almost physically painful to think his path might cross with Diego's. She'd dreamt of Diego and of El Valderon every night since she'd left. Left in a whirl of outrage, refusing to listen to so much as a solitary word from Diego. She'd known that if she'd stopped and listened to him she might have done what she always did—tried to craft herself into yet another person she wasn't in order to make someone happy.

Her hands slipped to her belly. She had someone else to prioritize now. That number one place was well and truly taken.

Wasn't there room enough for two?

It was difficult to admit, but with each day that passed she missed him more and more. She realized half the accusations she'd flung at him had been to protect herself from the truth. Life wasn't perfect. People weren't perfect. He, like her, was fallible. He made mistakes. She made mistakes.

And she loved him with every cell in her body.

Mary tipped her head to her shoulder and gave Isla a sidelong look. "Did you speak with your father today?"

She shook her head. "Not yet, but, you know... We had some really good talks before he left. Going through everything we did has kind of forced us to be more open with each other. More honest."

"I think your father is definitely president of the Isla MacLeay Fan Club!"

"Ach, away!" Isla laughed as a flush of pleasure hit her cheeks.

She had never felt more close to her father than she did now. There had definitely been a strong hit of *déjà vu* when she'd returned to Loch Craggen in tears about a man, but this time—this time she wasn't questioning her personal worth. Wasn't desperate for her father's approval. She now knew she'd had it all along.

And now she'd had a few long walks along the bracing Scottish coastline with her dad she knew in her heart that she had always been loved. Her parents, as she had begun to suspect, simply hadn't fit the traditional mold.

"What do you say you come out and walk

some of the dogs with me today? Give your eyes a rest." Mary held up a handful of dog leashes.

A bit of fresh air was exactly what she needed after two hours staring at the computer. And maybe an opportunity for the North Sea wind to blow away the cobwebs. Remind her that, with or without Diego, her future had changed for the better. Even heartache had its place in making a person better, and she was going to strive to give her child the best life she could.

She pulled on the cardigan lying on the end of her bed. "I don't suppose you have any top tips on how to become pack leader?"

Mary shot her a mischievous smile and beckoned for Isla to join her. "Plenty. How do you think I snared your father?"

Isla was still laughing as they rounded the corner. Mary's dogs were hilarious. She'd have to work a walk into her daily routine. And not only was her father's new girlfriend funny, she always seemed to have a new angle to look at a situation from.

Like the whole family issue. She'd suggested Isla remember that family came in all shapes and forms. Some were so-called traditional. A mum. A dad. Two-point-two children. And others…? Others were made up of people who loved and cared for you.

"Like Rufus," she'd said, pointing to her St

Bernard. "He's always on hand when I need a bit of a blub. Never tells me to bog off. Never tells me I'm being an idiot. He just lets me cry out whatever it is I'm boo-hooing about and all he wants in return is a belly-rub."

Leaving Mary to wrangle the dogs, Isla turned toward home. Her hands slipped to her tummy—which gave an enormous flip when she looked up at the front door to the cottage.

"Diego!" Isla's cheeks, pink with the cold, turned pale. "What are you doing here?"

All six-foot-something of him turned around, his dark eyes making the same powerful impact on her they had the first time all those weeks ago on El Valderon.

"I've come to try and convince my wife to come back home."

Isla looked down at her bare hand. She'd left the ring on the bedside table before she'd stormed off in a sea of hormones and self-protection.

"Convince or strong-arm?"

He winced.

"I'm sorry." She shook her head. "I— This is—"

"I know. It's a bit of a shock. But I'm not here to force you to do anything. I was just hoping… hoping you might spare a weary traveler a cup of coffee?"

It was so good to see him. So difficult not to run

straight into his arms. But her hands were clasped on her belly for a very specific reason. They were protecting the child she knew he didn't want.

Mary rounded the corner, holding a Chihuahua in each hand. They were her two "house dogs." The rest of the pack lived in Mary's luxury kennels just down the lane.

Her eyes widened when she saw Diego. "Isla? Everything all right, dearie?"

"Yes, I—" She threw a look at Mary. One that she hoped said *Can you just remind me of all of those pack leader tips again?*

"You know…" Mary's brow crinkled. "I just remembered I've got to go do a few things at the kennels. Is it all right if I catch up with you and your friend later? As long as you're okay?"

Isla looked at Diego, then back at Mary. She'd never been frightened of Diego. Ever. What she had been frightened of was her feelings for him. The powerlessness she'd felt when she had tried to change herself to make someone love her. She knew now that you couldn't *make* anyone love you. They either did or they didn't. And the fact that she was pregnant had been a game-changer for the pair of them.

"It's okay, Mary. We'll be fine."

A few minutes later, after a lot of faffing about with cups and kettles, coffee and her ever-present mint tea, Isla and Diego were sitting at the round wooden kitchen table in the window nook that faced out to the North Sea.

"If you threw a few palm trees about the place it'd be just like El Valderon," Diego said dryly.

"Ha! Yes. Exactly."

They both stared at their hot drinks for a moment, then as one began speaking.

"You first," he said.

"No, no. You've come the furthest." Isla lifted her steaming mug to her lips and nodded for him to go ahead.

"I—"

Dios! This was harder than he'd thought it would be. All the speeches he'd prepared at home, on the plane, on the drive here…were gone. Every last word.

"Diego?"

"I love you."

She pursed her lips. "That may be so, but you don't want a child and I do, so—"

He held up a finger. "Please. Hear me out."

"Did my father put you up to this? Tell you that you had to make an honest woman of me?"

"No." Diego gave an amazed laugh. "Quite the opposite, in fact."

"What?"

Pure indignation lit up Isla's features and Diego couldn't help but smile. There she was.

The spirited woman he'd fallen head over heels in love with.

"Honesty is the best policy?"

Isla nodded, though a flash of concern blunted the purity of her blue eyes for a moment.

"I love you."

"You already said that, and I told you—"

He spoke over her. "And I want to be a father to my child. To our children…if you'll have me."

"Oh? So now all of a sudden, after one month on your own and an entire adulthood of swearing off procreation, you've decided you want to have a big family? What spurred this on?"

He could see it was bluster. That she was protecting herself. The child. *Their* child.

"Por favor, amorcita." He took her hands in his and drew them to his lips. "I promise—once you agree to marry me again, for real—you can lead all of our conversations, but…if you will let me… I'd like to explain why I was such a *huevón."*

"I don't know what that means," she said with a sniff.

"It means I've not only been an idiot but I dropped the ball when it was most important. To us. It isn't as if you got pregnant on your own."

"Or on purpose," she added.

Her hands swept across her belly and a soft, beautiful smile lit up her face.

"Whatever you're about to say, Diego, know this. I am over the moon that I'm pregnant."

She didn't look elated. But she did look determined.

"I *want* this baby," she said, her index fingers arrowed at her flat belly.

"And I want it too."

"But you were so adamant…"

"That was before. When anger and revenge fueled everything. With Axl dying the way he did—everything happening so fast—it was all too much to process. There were too many sea changes to make on the edge of a coin."

She fixed him with a *yeah, right* glare.

"I did change. From the moment I met you—"

"All soaked in blood and surf and dirt? Yeah. A real pretty picture."

"You were then and still are the most beautiful woman in the world, Isla. And I would love for you to come home. To *our* home."

"Having a child is a huge thing. Particularly when you don't even want one to sit on your lap!"

It was his turn to feel sheepish. "She asked for you instead of me. I didn't want to admit it. I was so busy fighting the fact I was in love with you I just let her request fuel the lie I'd fed myself over the years."

"Which was…?"

"That I wasn't fit to be a father. That I was a

man who couldn't be trusted to be there when it counted."

She blinked a few times, as if reliving a memory, then asked, "And what was it that changed your mind?"

"Paz."

Her eyebrows shot up. "Paz Cruz?"

"The one and only. Believe it or not, he and I have had quite a few heart-to-hearts over the past few weeks and it's got me thinking. If the son of a man who was so obviously on the wrong side of the law could raise a child who's so kind—so willing to give of himself—maybe I'm better equipped than I thought to take that risk. So long as I let go of my anger over my brother's death—the self-hatred that I wasn't there."

"And…?" Isla reached across to him, gave his hand a squeeze. "Have you done that? Forgiven yourself?"

He nodded. "Yes—and no. I will always wish I'd been there. There will never be a day that I won't. But…" He looked her straight in the eye. "Knowing I have you by my side would always give me strength."

For the first time since he'd reached into his chest and handed her his heart she smiled. That full, bright, cheery smile that lit her up from within.

"What do you think? Could you leave the wilds of Loch Craggen behind a second time?"

"For you?" Isla feigned having to think about it, then threw herself into his arms. "For you I would do *anything*. Well…" She pulled back and gave him a serious look. "I will never eat beetroot. I can tell you that here and now."

"Right. Got it. I promise." He crossed his heart. "No beetroot. Can I kiss my wife now?"

"You may."

The moment their lips met he knew he would do everything in his power to make Isla happy. To bring her and their children joy. Peace was still a fragile thing on the island of El Valderon, but it lived solidly and happily in his heart.

EPILOGUE

"I CAN'T BELIEVE how many there are!" Isla tucked her hand in the crook of Diego's arm and gave his shoulder a kiss as they stood side by side to watch the excitement on the beach.

"There are over three hundred, if the last count was accurate." Diego pointed toward the shore-line, where the baby turtles were being released into the sea. "Look at your father. He's absolutely over the moon!"

Isla laughed. "This is pure bliss for him. Having his family all together..."

She leaned toward the baby Diego had strapped to his chest in the El Valderon version of a baby sling and gave his dark curly head a kiss.

"Hola, mi amor!"

Her heart nearly burst with happiness as her brand-new son wrapped his tiny hand round her index finger.

Diego slipped his arm round his wife's shoulders and dropped a soft kiss on to her forehead.

"This is all because of you."

She pursed her lips together and laughed.

"Rubbish! It was *you*. You and Paz, working tirelessly to bring peace and stability to El Valderon."

They both looked at Serena, a mother clearly bursting with pride as her son talked a large group of school children through the release.

Paz was wearing his paramedic uniform, his long trousers rolled up to his knees as he and the children each brought a baby sea turtle close to the shoreline and watched it make its way toward the sea.

Diego tipped his head to the side, his cheeky grin lighting up her insides every bit as much as seeing him the first time had. "Shall we agree that it is because of all of us?"

She gave him a light kiss. "I can agree with that."

Diego slipped his hand to his wife's back and gave it a light rub. Isla shimmied against it. His touch never failed to unleash a flight of butterflies.

"I love you, Isla." His voice was thick with emotion.

Another ribbon of heat twirled through her belly and swirled round her heart. "I love you, too." She meant it with all her soul. "Meeting you…albeit in some rather peculiar circumstances…" They shared a wry laugh. "Meeting you changed how I saw things. How I saw the world. Life."

Diego brushed the backs of his fingers along his wife's cheek. "You give me too much credit. Besides…" He protectively cupped his newborn's head with his hand. "I don't think I'd be a proud father of two, watching just about the whole of El Valderon come together to secure a peaceful future for everyone who lives here, without you."

Isla threw back her head and laughed. "We're in danger of becoming a mutual admiration society if we don't watch it!"

Diego's eyes dropped to half-mast as he swept his hand along Isla's back, then gave her a saucy pat on the butt. "Oh, we are long past that, *mi amor. Long* past that."

Isla's lips parted in a wide smile. "I think we may have to find time for that *siesta* we spoke about this morning after all…"

Diego's tongue swept across his lower lip. "I think that is a very good idea."

Emilio ran up the beach from where he'd been standing with his grandfather and Mary—who, she noticed, was wearing an engagement ring. Isla crossed her fingers that she and Diego would be on the receiving end of a bit of a speech and a toast at their anniversary dinner tonight.

Two years! It had gone by so quickly that sometimes she thought she'd barely drawn a breath. And other times…when her husband pulled his fingers through her hair and lifted her face to meet his gaze, his lips…she felt as if she'd finally learnt how to make a moment truly stand still.

Emilio reached up and grabbed his mother's hand. "Mamá! Turtles!"

She scooped her son up into her arms and laughed. "You want to set one of the babies free?"

Her toddler nodded, his grin of anticipation nearly splitting his face in two. Of course he did. She did as well.

"What do you say we all go down and help?"

"Sounds good to me!"

Diego took his wife's hand and together, as a family, they walked to the shoreline to join their community as they celebrated the first successful—and peaceful—release.

* * * * *

If you enjoyed this story, check out these other great reads from Annie O'Neil

Tempted By Her Single Dad Boss
The Army Doc's Christmas Angel
One Night with Dr. Nikolaides
Reunited with Her Parisian Surgeon

All available now!